For Isabella!

THE 9 LIVES

⚬ of ⚬

ALEXANDER BADDENFIELD

by

JOHN BEMELMANS MARCIANO

illustrated by

SOPHIE BLACKALL

Sophie Blackall

PUFFIN BOOKS
An Imprint of Penguin Group (USA)

PUFFIN BOOKS
Published by the Penguin Group
Penguin Group (USA) LLC
375 Hudson Street
New York, New York 10014

USA * Canada * UK * Ireland * Australia
New Zealand * India * South Africa * China

penguin.com
A Penguin Random House Company

First published in the United States of America by Viking,
an imprint of Penguin Young Readers Group, 2013
Published by Puffin Books, an imprint of Penguin Young Readers Group, 2014

Copyright © 2013 by John Bemelmans Marciano
Illustrations copyright © 2013 by Sophie Blackall

Penguin supports copyright. Copyright fuels creativity, encourages diverse voices, pro-
motes free speech, and creates a vibrant culture. Thank you for buying an authorized
edition of this book and for complying with copyright laws by not reproducing, scanning,
or distributing any part of it in any form without permission. You are supporting writers
and allowing Penguin to continue to publish books for every reader.

THE LIBRARY OF CONGRESS HAS CATALOGED THE VIKING EDITION AS FOLLOWS:
Marciano, John Bemelmans.
The 9 lives of Alexander Baddenfield / by John Bemelmans Marciano.
pages cm
Summary: Twelve-year-old Alexander Baddenfield, the last in a long line of evil men
who die young, has his cat's extra eight lives transplanted into his own body,
while his caretaker, Winterbottom, strives to keep him safe.
ISBN: 978-0-670-01406-4 (hardcover)
[1. Conduct of life—Fiction. 2. Death—Fiction. 3. Reincarnation—Fiction.
4. Wealth—Fiction. 5. Orphans—Fiction. 6. Cats—Fiction. 7. Humorous stories.]
I. Title. II. Title: Nine lives of Alexander Baddenfield.
PZ7.M328556Aah 2013
[Fic]—dc23
2012048448

Puffin Books ISBN 978-0-14-751233-8

Printed in the United States of America

1 3 5 7 9 10 8 6 4 2

For Dan
—*J.B.M.*

For Jack
Kilkelly-Schmidt
—*S.B.*

The Grave
of
ALEXANDER BADDENFIELD

 grave should be a sad thing, and the grave of a child the saddest thing of all. The tombstone reads:

Here Lies Alexander Baddenfield,
Who Departed This Mortal Coil after a Dozen Years.
He Was the Last of the Baddenfields—*Thank God!!!*

That last part isn't chiseled into the granite. Instead, it's scrawled across the headstone in spray paint.

A man has come to visit the grave. Winterbottom is his name. In one hand he carries a tulip plant, in the other a black bag. Winterbottom places the flowerpot on the grave, then reaches into his bag, takes out a rag and a can of paint remover, and carefully wipes off the graffiti. "Only one scrawl on the headstone today. That's pretty good," he tells himself.

his is all that remains in the world for this young

o do, as Winterbottoms have served Baddenfields

since time immemorial. *Why* they have done so is a
question every Winterbottom must have asked himself
every day of his life. Or perhaps never. Maybe that's the
only way they could stand to work for that horrid family.

Other than graffiti artists, Winterbottom is the only
person ever to have come to pay respects to Alexander, his funeral included. How is it possible, you ask,
that only ONE person could show up to the funeral of a
twelve-year-old boy? Could anyone really have been so
bad in so few years?

The short answer is yes.

But now you say to yourself, "Aha! I know: The twist
is that the boy is not really dead. It says it right there in
the title—Alexander has nine lives. He will be reborn,
again and again, so that by his ninth life this awful child
will have learned his lesson. His heart will fill with
love for his fellow man, and he will become a Not-So-
Baddenfield, or even a Goodenfield, and he will turn all
his money over to the poor and dedicate his final life to
charitable good works."

If this were a Hollywood movie, or a fairy tale, or a
run-of-the-mill chapter book, this would undoubtedly be
the case. But in the real world such things rarely happen. The truth of the matter is that Alexander Badden-

field used up all nine of his lives without the least bit of remorse or redemption, because Alexander Baddenfield only ever cared about one thing: himself. And that, dear friends, is the most Baddenfield trait of them all.

But who were these Baddenfields? If you care to know the story of the boy, you must first know the story of his family, for Alexander belonged to the most curious, the most singular, the most dastardly clan ever to sully this blue and green earth.

The Lives
of
BADDENFIELDS

To say that the Baddenfield family had a checkered past is to insult innocent board games everywhere. It is also inaccurate. The lives of the Baddenfields were not checkered. If their family tree were a chessboard, the squares would all be black.

The Baddenfields were Dutch. This might surprise you, as you probably think of the Dutch as a smiley, round-faced folk responsible mainly for windmills, waffles, and wooden clogs, but in fact the people of the Netherlands are a far more crafty lot than that, especially when it comes to making money. In fact, they created capitalism, on or about the date of March 31, 1624. Among the first people to take to the new idea was one Nikolas Boddenveld.

Like most of the Dutch people, Nikolas Boddenveld emerged out of the lowland swamps, although out of which precise swamp no one can tell. He did this alongside his servant Winderboddem, or rather a few steps behind Winderboddem, who was scouting ahead for any dangerous holes Nikolas might fall into. Their two families had already cohabited for countless generations, and a peculiar sort of evolution had occurred between them, as with that kind of little fish that evolved to pick the food out of the teeth of a much bigger species of fish that would have died of cavities without the little fish. The Winderboddems, you see, had evolved into the most careful and care-giving people ever known, enabling the Boddenvelds to become the most careless and uncaring.

Along with creating capitalism, the Dutch also created the first great capitalist disaster. Or rather, Nikolas Boddenveld did.

The Great Tulip Bubble of 1637 is the most studied financial panic of all time. Basically, a few tulip bulbs from Turkey showed up in Holland one day and everybody went wild for them. If you wanted to be one of the well-to-do, you had to have tulips; if you didn't have tulips, you weren't any better than the dirt they were planted in. Perfectly normal people began buying up tulip bulbs at any

price, and the more people bought them, the more expensive they became, because there were only so many bulbs to go around. The bulbs eventually got to costing more than what most folks made in a year. One poor sailor, fresh off the boat from the New World and never having seen one before, mistook a tulip bulb in his boss's office for an onion and ate it. Unable to pay for it, the sailor was thrown in jail and locked away.*

Hearing the tale of the unlucky sailor, Nikolas Boddenveld had a great idea. He went around to markets buying up onions to resell as tulip bulbs, at a slightly lower price than anyone else was selling them for. Pretty soon, there were more tulip bulbs than anyone knew what to do with, and they became worthless. People who had spent their life's savings on the promise of a flower were put into the poorhouse. "Which is precisely where they belong for being so stupid," said an amused Nikolas Boddenveld to his man Winderboddem. Winderboddem, however, thought that the promise of a flower sounded like a perfectly fine thing to spend a life's savings on.

The badness of the Boddenvelds could scarcely be boxed into so small a country as Holland, and so the six sons of Nikolas took to the seven seas, with the six sons of Winderboddem by their sides. They first became privateers (a legal kind of pirate) and then colonialists (which is the same thing, but on land). Dutch seamen,

* This story is actually true. (Maybe.)

you see, settled the world, establishing colonies in South Africa and South America, as well as the island archipelagos of the East and West Indies. The branch of Baddenfields that most interests us, however, settled in the upper eastern stretches of North America.

Did you know New York was once called New Amsterdam? You probably have heard that the island of Manhattan was bought for $24 in beads and such, but did you know who did the buying? Pieter Boddenveld.

Chopping up his purchase into parcels, Pieter resold the island piece by tiny piece—at a massive profit—to his arriving countrymen, who went about digging canals and constructing windmills and in general making the place look as much like Holland as possible. The descendents of the settlers of New Amsterdam were called Knickerbockers, the most famous of whom was Rip Van Winkle. Rip slept for twenty years after his cider got spiked with a massive dose of knockout drops by Pieter Boddenveld's son, Pieter Jr. (Or rather, by Winderboddem Jr., at little Pieter's behest.) He did it for no other reason than to play a mean trick, but it was *so* mean no one else could even conceive of it, and everybody assumed that Rip had taken a twenty-year nap just because he was lazy, including Rip himself.

These were awful things, but then the Boddenvelds always did awful things, and for the same motives as the two Pieters: money and meanness. But it was when

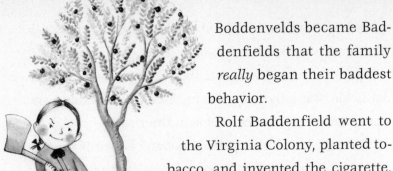

Boddenvelds became Baddenfields that the family *really* began their baddest behavior.

Rolf Baddenfield went to the Virginia Colony, planted tobacco, and invented the cigarette. His descendant Weems Baddenfield cut down a cherry tree on the nearby Washington plantation and blackmailed his little playmate Georgie into taking the fall for it.

At the Boston Tea Party, the patriots made sure it was Baddenfield Tea they dumped into the harbor, after which wily Quincy Baddenfield drained the harbor, bottled the water, and invented iced tea, which he sold at two bits a pop.

Every Baddenfield alive voted against Abraham Lincoln, and some dead ones too. Twice.

The Baddenfields were slave owners and strike-breakers, strip miners and sweatshop operators, and they referred to the Great Depression as the Great Happiness.

There was only *one* good thing about the Baddenfields: They didn't live very long. They also tended to die in particularly grisly and poetically justified ways.

This manner of dying went back at least as far as Niko-

las Boddenveld, who confused his flowers with his onions and wound up chopping a tulip bulb into some tuna salad and having a massive allergic reaction. He blew up into a red, bloated ball, rolled away into a nearby canal, and floated out to sea, never to be heard from again.

Pieter Boddenveld was shot to death by a much savvier and angrier tribe of Indians from whom he tried to buy Canada for a buck fifty's worth of purple ribbon and a jar of sauerkraut, while Pieter Jr. passed away from a cracked skull after tripping over Rip Van Winkle's beard.

The only reason the generations continued at all was on account of the carefulness of the Winterbottoms. But even a whole gaggle of Winterbottoms couldn't save the Baddenfields from themselves when they all got together, as you will shortly discover.

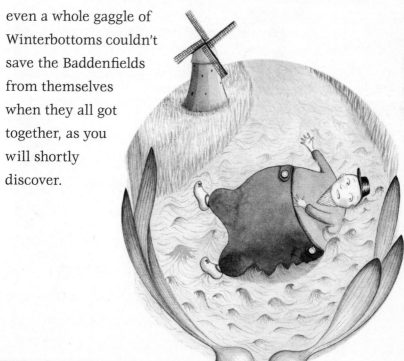

Baddenfield
Family
REUNION

This group photo is the sole memento of the ill-fated holiday that all but wiped the Baddenfields off the face of the earth. It also marks the first and only time that all the different branches of the family got together in one place. If you take out a magnifying glass, you will notice a baby carriage in the back left corner of the picture. The two tiny hands reaching out of it belong to Alexander, and the gawky older boy standing next to him is the Winterbottom you met at the opening of our book.

The reason for the gathering was a safari organized by Smuts Baddenveld, last of the Afrikaner branch of the family. A famed poacher, Smuts had gathered on his game preserve the most endangered animals in the world for one great hunting expedition. The prizes would not be trophies but the honor of making a species go extinct.

However, it was the Baddenfields themselves who were about to go extinct, or nearly.

First to go was Smuts himself, who contracted a lethal form of spotted fever from a rare Beringo giraffe he had kidnapped from the Pretoria Zoo. Things only got worse from there.

Juan Baddenvaldez of the Suriname branch of the clan had a clear shot at the last three black pygmy rhinoceroses in the world, a mama rhino and her two calves, but he got so excited he shot himself in the foot while taking out his gun. The rhino mama charged him, and though he hobbled away as fast as he could, Juan couldn't escape getting gored to death on her horn. His faithful servant, Wintergomez, tried to save him, but alas, he too was gored, not once but twice, by each of the rhino babies.

Why did the other Baddenfields not rush in to help their relative? They were too busy laughing. Budi Baddenfeltro of the Indonesian side of the family perhaps regretted this behavior in the final moments of his own life. Tracking the rarest of bok, the bontebok, Budi ventured far into the bush, assuming the deerlike animals posed no threat to him. What he didn't reckon on, however, was that a pride of lions that had been stalking the herd all day would decide that Budi and his Winterbottomtro would make a far tenderer meal than any bok.

Fat Oskar von Baddenveld of the German branch of the family watched the whole thing through a pair of binoculars and snickered at his cousin's dismemberment while eating little links of sausages like popcorn. Shortly thereafter, the last living herd of African forest elephants stampeded and stomped him to death, as his greasy fingers kept slipping off the trigger of his rifle.

The giggles and laughter that attended Oskar's demise were somewhat quieter, on account of how few Baddenfields remained. Still, Jimbo Badden-day-o of the Caribbean side of the clan wasn't about to let the misfortunes of his distant relatives get in the way of his killing the last surviving mouse-faced chimpanzee, which he had cornered. What he failed to appreciate was the intelligence of this particular primate, which had recovered Oskar von Baddenveld's rifle and wiped off the grease, and now used it to shoot Jimbo.

At this point, you might begin to feel sorry for Alexander's father, the last of the hunting party and thus, along with his son, the last of the Baddenfields. Alexander Sr. had created the Urban Tankmobile, a vehicle that took up three lanes of highway, averaged fourteen feet per gallon, and went on to become the bestselling car in America in the opening years of the twenty-first century. He was the richest Baddenfield who had ever lived, and also the meanest. His idea of fun was to sit around

the breakfast table reading the obituaries and cackling with laughter. But he wasn't laughing now. This far out in the bush, his and his son's only hopes for survival were Winterbottom Sr. and his twelve-year-old son, Winterbottom Jr., themselves now the last of their line.

It had gotten dark. And cold. Shivering, starving, and scared, the little group hiked their way back to base camp by moonlight. Arriving as dawn broke, they had just begun to relax when, suddenly, a hungry beast poked its head out of the mess tent. It was the rarest animal in the history of rare animals: the king African snow cheetah. A gleam came into Alexander Sr.'s eye as he raised his rifle. "The pelt of that animal will look positively *capital* in my study!"

"Don't do it, sir," Winterbottom Sr. whispered. "Don't you see? Fate is punishing you Baddenfields for trying to kill these animals. Pulling that trigger would be suicide!"

Winterbottom Sr. was right, although the shot itself went off without a hitch. It missed, however, due to the lousy aim of Alexander's father, and succeeded only in alerting the cheetah to their presence. Terrified, Alexander's father leapt into his Tankmobile and sped off. Winterbottom Sr. turned to his son and said, "Save the baby!" and ran after the vehicle.

A Winterbottom to the core, the prudent young man draped himself over Alexander's carriage and pretend-

ed to be dead. The confused cheetah sniffed the limp twelve-year-old, tapped him with his paw, and, getting no reaction, moved on.

Winterbottom wheeled his young charge along in the tracks of their fathers, both of which abruptly ended in the same place, a few hundred feet past a run-over, broken sign that read, WARNING! QUICKSAND!

Floating on top of a quicksand bog was a pocket watch and a license plate: BADD1. Alexander's father had loved that vanity plate, even if he couldn't read it, never having learned how. Too much work. Winterbottom could well imagine the elder Baddenfield barreling over the sign and sinking, and his own father jumping in to try to save him. Crying, the boy fished his father's pocket watch out of the bog and swore that he would be the first Winterbottom to keep a Baddenfield from the curse of dying young.

He would fail nine times.

The First Life
of
ALEXANDER BADDENFIELD

Cutting through Chinatown across the lower fifth of Manhattan is Canal Street, which got its name from having been built over the longest canal of New Amsterdam. Baddenfield Castle looms over the corner of Bouwerie Lane, separated from the sidewalk by the last remaining section of old canal. This moat protected generations of Baddenfields from those who would do them harm. For the same reason, what had been built in 1643 as a windmill and cottage had over the years morphed into a watchtower and castle.

Alexander grew up in a kind of lockdown, surrounded by the battlements, barbed wire, and spy cameras of his family stronghold. The greatest measure of security, however, came in the form of Winterbottom himself. So obsessed was Winterbottom with the thought that nothing bad should happen to the last of the Badden-

fields that he hardly let Alexander do anything at all.

Some of his precautions were the kind we all learn. Winterbottom instructed Alexander to look left before he crossed the street, then right, then back left again. Like many a parent, he smeared the boy with so much sunblock he could've passed for a ghost. But Winterbottom always took things one step further. Even when Alexander was old enough to sit in the front of the car, Winterbottom insisted he remain in the back, strapped into his booster seat. Wary of food allergies, he kept Alexander on the most restricted of diets. "Remember your ancestor Nikolas, who died from eating an onion," Winterbottom would say (no matter that it was actually a tulip bulb). No nuts, no milk, no cheese, no ice cream, no bread, no pasta, no soy, no shellfish, no eggs, and absolutely, positively *no* onions.

Winterbottom was so nervous that what little he allowed Alexander to eat he always tested himself first. How could he know the boy's meal wasn't contaminated with E. coli or salmonella or some other fiendish bacteria? Or that it wasn't poisoned by one of the Baddenfields' many enemies? (And he wasn't just being paranoid—on several occasions, Winterbottom *was* hospitalized for poisoning!)

Through Winterbottom's best efforts and the boy having been orphaned at so young an age, Alexander should have become the first decent human being his miserable

family had ever produced. Should have, but didn't. Nastiness was intertwined with the Baddenfield DNA. That, plus Alexander was just too filthy rich. It's hard to be good when you're rich, and Alexander was quite possibly the richest person on earth, having inherited not just his father's money, but the money of all the Baddenfields who had ever lived.

So how bad was Alexander?

Alexander always wanted to be a bully. When, on the first day of kindergarten, he realized he was the smallest kid in class and thus unable to beat anybody up, he paid a couple of second-graders to do the job for him.

Alexander kept a water pistol filled with ketchup to squirt at anyone who annoyed him. The thing was, most everything anyone else did annoyed him. Being nice annoyed him. Being grateful annoyed him. Saying thank you annoyed him. Holding the door open for people annoyed him. Being happy annoyed him. Being sad annoyed him.

Alexander littered *everywhere*.

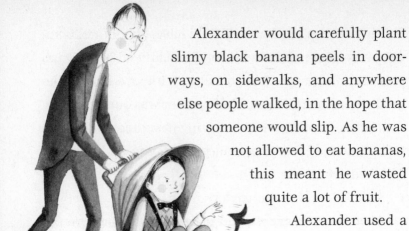

Alexander would carefully plant slimy black banana peels in doorways, on sidewalks, and anywhere else people walked, in the hope that someone would slip. As he was not allowed to eat bananas, this meant he wasted quite a lot of fruit.

Alexander used a stroller until he was eight, because why walk when someone will roll you? The only reason he stopped was that people began to think he was in a wheelchair and kept coming up trying to be nice to him. He went through a lot of ketchup that way.

Alexander wore diapers until the age of nine. It was a lot of effort to wipe his own behind, and a dirty job besides.

When he was ten, Alexander quit school. "What's there to learn when you're already rich?"

Alexander even poisoned his own meals, sending Winterbottom to the hospital on several occasions.

The older Alexander got, the less Winterbottom could control him. He would attempt to coax Alexander back to school, pointing out that his father's same attitude

had left him unable to read the WARNING! QUICKSAND! sign. Alexander noted that (a) he could read and (b) his father's mistake had been leaving Winterbottom Sr. behind, a point Winterbottom Jr. could hardly argue.

The story of the safari always made Alexander sad. Not because of the grisly deaths of his father and relatives. He was quite glad to be rid of them, seeing as he had inherited everything they owned. No, what grieved him was that in the tale lay the proof that Baddenfields always died young and with their just deserts.

At his twelfth birthday party, Alexander couldn't manage to enjoy himself. Partly it may have been the twelve unlit candles that stood on his cake—Winterbottom wouldn't allow any real fire in the house—and partly that his only guests were his cat, his driver Sam, and Winterbottom. But his real agitation came from the grim facts he confronted on the plaques below his ancestors' portraits in the Hall of Baddenfields:

ROLF BADDENFIELD

who died from smoke inhalation, October 3rd, 1616, aged 24.

WEEMS BADDENFIELD

who choked on a cherry pit, February 22nd, 1749, aged 17.

QUINCY BADDENFIELD

who froze to death selling ice cubes to soldiers at Valley Forge, February 19th, 1778, aged 26.

It wasn't that Alexander feared dying. The boy's single good attribute was his bravery. In fact, Alexander daydreamed of the dramatic ways in which he might meet—or better yet, cheat—death. What upset Alexander was that he only had one short life to live and that, by his family's standards, it was already half over.

All this made Alexander particularly resentful of his cat.

"Life is totally unfair," he told his pet, who was rubbing up against his leg and purring. "You are nothing but a worthless cat, whose best day is taken up by twenty-three and a half hours of naps, while I am richer than rich and want to do things you can't even imagine. But you get to have nine lives, and I get only one."

His cat, whose name was Shaddenfrood, purred louder.

Alexander brooded over this injustice until, in a flash of spectacular self-interest that only the mind of a Baddenfield was capable of, he hit upon his Great Idea.

"Winterbottom!" Alexander yelled.

Winterbottom, who was in the middle of making a flourless, cheeseless, tomatoless pizza, dropped everything and raced down eight flights of stairs to make sure nothing was wrong. "Yes," he panted, "Alex," he panted, "ander," he panted.

"What took you so long, Winterbottom? I have had a Great Idea."

"A great idea?"

"*No,*" he corrected him. "A Great Idea."

"Ah, I see—a Great Idea. And how can I help with this Great Idea?"

"Call Dr. Sorrow," Alexander said, rubbing his hands together.

"Dr. Sorrow!" Winterbottom gasped, terrified something really was wrong. "Do you have a fever? Is it foot-and-mouth disease? Was it the eggless omelet I made you this morning?"

"Just call the doctor," Alexander said, unnecessarily, as Winterbottom had already hit the SORROW icon on his phone.

Dr. Alfred August Sorrow was the greatest doctor in the world. He had restored sight to the blind, provided tans to albinos, and made the legless walk, and for these and other outstanding accomplishments he had been award-ed the Nobel Prize for Doctoring a record seven times.

Dr. Sorrow had first treated Alexander as a baby, when Winterbottom had brought him to the office, con-vinced that he had contracted some horrible disease or another while on safari. More than once the doctor had cursed himself for having taken the boy on as a patient, as the Baddenfield clan represented everything he de-tested. But how could he hold a baby responsible for the

sins of his family? Of course, the boy had grown into every inch a Baddenfield.

So it was with a frown that Dr. Sorrow answered Winterbottom's call. "What is it this time?" he said to Alexander's hypochondriacal caretaker.

"Please don't hang up on me, Dr. Sorrow! It's urgent this time! I swear to you it is!"

"You know the office hours. I know you know them, because I tell them to you every time you call. They are—"

"I think he is dying, Doctor." There was muffled fumbling of the phone. "Yes, Alexander is definitely dying."

Dr. Sorrow sighed and hung up, not bothering to argue since he knew he'd wind up going to Baddenfield Castle anyway. He would at least do it slowly. And by subway.

The Canal Street stop of the Z train let Dr. Sorrow off at the corner of the castle. As he rang the bell and waited for the drawbridge to lower over the moat, he looked up at the gloomy brick monstrosity and wondered what it would be like to be so utterly filthy rich.

Winterbottom, as always, was there waiting for him. "Come in, come in," he said. The doctor shuddered walking through the creepy hallway with all the portraits, and again when the elevator deposited him on the top floor of the castle, in the tower that was Alexander's room. The boy was sitting in a chair stroking his cat, like some sort of junior varsity James Bond villain. He

hardly looked sick. In fact, he looked as healthy as a boy could. Then again, he always did.

"What is it?" Dr. Sorrow asked, although it sounded less like a question and more like an accusation.

"Hello to you too, Doctor," Alexander said.

"What is it?" Dr. Sorrow said again. "Do you have a fever?"

"Oh, I'm not sick in the least," he said. "What I want is to offer you the opportunity to go down in history as the greatest doctor ever."

Dr. Sorrow, pretty much sure he'd go down in history as the greatest doctor ever regardless, asked what Alexander meant by that.

"What do you *mean* by that, Alexander?"

"What I mean is, I have a Great Idea." He paused for dramatic effect. "I want you to surgically remove the nine lives from a common house cat and implant them into me. *This* common house cat," Alexander said, and squeezed Shaddenfrood.

The cat went *Meow!*

"And if the cat doesn't make it through the operation," Alexander said, "well, that's a price I'm willing to pay."

Meow! Shaddenfrood again went.

The proposal shocked Dr. Sorrow. He'd been prepared for something insane, but this was too much! "You . . . you rotten boy, you!" he sputtered. "I am not proud of having been your doctor, but I have been bound by my Hippo-

cratic oath to do my best to save the life of anyone who is my patient. But this! This is not saving a life! This is giving you eight more! This so-called 'great idea' of yours."

It irked Alexander that the doctor failed to appreciate his Great Idea, but he still wanted to convince him. "Look, Doc, have a little bit of vision. I'm presenting you with the opportunity to make medical history here."

"The only opportunity is for malpractice! Such an operation would be immoral, not to mention impossible!" Dr. Sorrow composed himself and sniffed. "Only a not-very-bright boy who quit school at far too young an age would ever come up with such a ludicrous idea."

Although Alexander may have been the meanest boy alive, he highly detested it when other people were mean to *him*. "Oh fine, you crotchety old quack!" he said. "Take yourself and your Noble Prizes and your Hypocritical oaths and get out of my house! You may be the first-best doctor in the world, but I'm going to find the second-, third-, and fourth-best doctors and hire them all! I will hire however many it takes to get what I want."

"I can assure you, young Baddenfield, that you will be hard-pressed to find *any* reputable physician willing to take on this 'great idea' of yours, let alone the second-, third-, or fourth-best doctor in the world." Dr. Sorrow bowed his head and said, "I am only glad that *I* no longer have to be in your service. Good day, and good-bye."

Winterbottom followed Dr. Sorrow all the way down

27

the winding staircase, begging him please, *please* not to quit, the boy was a Baddenfield, and surely, sooner rather than later, he would get deathly ill and only the great Dr. Sorrow would be able to save him. Before he finished walking across the planks of the drawbridge over the moat, the doctor paused. He quite strongly was attached to that Hippocratic oath of his, and it really didn't let him fire a patient, no matter how awful.

"If anything is ever *truly* wrong with the boy," Dr. Sorrow said, stepping onto the sidewalk, "call me."

A. A. Sorrow, MD, may have been the greatest doctor ever, but he was lousy when it came to judging the morality of his fellow physicians. As it happened, it was easy to find doctors willing to do anything Alexander asked, so long as he was willing to pay them gobs of cash to do it. The problem was that all of them, to a man and to a woman, were baffled as to how to accomplish the surgical feat in question.

Crisscrossing the world in the family Boeingfield 999, Alexander and Winterbottom went far and farther down the Best Doctors in the World list they had printed out from Wikipedia, until Alexander had gotten sick of hearing the same answer over and over.

"Doctors! They're no use at all!" Alexander said, walk-

ing out of the Zurich office of the twelfth-best one and ripping up the list. "No more doctors!"

"It's all for the best," said Winterbottom, who had been trying to stop Alexander's scheme from the start. "Even if you were to find a doctor who believed that cats have nine lives, transplanting them would be too risky a procedure to perform on *you*. The last of the Baddenfields should not be treated as a guinea pig!"

"I'm not giving up," Alexander said. "Now I need nine extra lives just to prove all these quacks are wrong."

Returning to America, Alexander had his pilot land in Readington, New Jersey, home of the largest drug companies in the world. Located here was the headquarters of Baddenfield Pharmaceutical, or—as it was affectionately known within the industry—BaddPharm, home of such wonder drugs as the Komadose® sleeping pill.

"The drug companies are the ones that do the research, Winterbottom," Alexander said. "They *invent* the medicine, so they're the ones that can get me my nine lives."

But the word in New Jersey was no better than it had been anywhere else.

"I'm afraid we only create drugs that treat diseases, Master Baddenfield, sir," said the Head Chairman of Executive Vice Presidents for BaddPharm. "We don't do anything that would actually make people healthier. That would be bad for business."

Alexander began to shake. His face went from pink to

red to purple. Foam formed at the corners of his mouth. He was about to have one of his Alexander Moments, which generally involved a string of third-person pronouncements and mortal threats. Winterbottom opened his mental umbrella and prepared for the storm.

"Alexander *Bad*denfield is unfamiliar with things not going his way.

"Alexander **Bad**denfield does not like the word 'no.'

"Alexander **BAD**denfield is going to start firing people.

"And worse."

An emergency meeting was called. All of the top research scientists from all of the departments of BaddPharm were summoned to the largest meeting room in the facility. The doors were locked, the windows covered over. On the whiteboard at the front of the room, the agenda was written out in black magic marker:

- AB wants 9 LIVES
- AB has CAT with 9 LIVES to GIVE
- HOW to TRANSPLANT 9L from CAT➔AB

All the assembled MSs and PhDs scratched at their notepads and tapped at their laptops, racking their brains for an answer.

One by one, the experts were asked to render their expert opinions, and one by one they obfuscated. "Obfuscate" is a big word that few understand; "to obfuscate" means "to use big words for the purpose of not being understood."

Here are some of those words.

TA[

INTRAVENA[

PARTICIPANTS *placebo* ERG[

DIACRITIC

opathies

infinite CONTRO[

STUDIES

EXOS[

[O]DITICALLY

effectively

[p]eycling

TRYPTOPHANY[

[he]moglobin *amino*

QUOTIDIAN HETE[R]

[M]ULTIFACTORIAL or POLY[

journals

[o]pomorphicizatio[n]

METRICS *IPSIS*

GENTIAL GENUS
folic organic neurofibri
CRYOGENICALLY
ALLY amorphous COSIN
FELINES psycho
GROUPS OUTCOME
OSES summatio
PLATEAL philherme
HREONYLPHENYLALANIN
UNLIKELY jargon
ZYGOUS autosomal
ENIC NONPOLYPOSIS
ACETYLCHOLINESTERASE
MITOCHONDRIAL
dialetically adenoidal
PIDEMIOLOG

When Alexander could take no more, he held up a hand and said, "Enough! If you all think you can confuse and bore me into going away, you're wrong. Is it too much to ask for you to solve *one* little problem? Is it going to be the think tank for all of you?" Normally, a think tank is a gathering of top minds; at BaddPharm, it was a literal steel tank that employees were locked into. "And no one gets out until someone gives me *something* that helps!"

"How about Dr. Graft?"

The name cracked the silence of the room like a bite of potato chips in a library. Everyone turned to look at who had said it, a low-level intern in the toe fungus department. "Oh," the man said sheepishly, and shrank down in his chair.

"Who?" Alexander said.

"Dr. Torvic Kranstenenif. 'Dr. Graft' was a bit of a—uh—playful nickname. But really, it is best not to speak of him," the Head Chairman of Executive Vice Presidents said in a nervous fidget. "He was a—well, I don't know *what* he was. A mad scientist, I suppose. He caused us a lot of trouble, and cost you a great deal of money."

"What did he do?" Alexander asked.

"He worked in our artificial limbs division. It's really a wonderful part of the company—giving arms and legs to people who don't have them. Profitable, very profitable." He smiled. "Mostly, we make fake limbs out of

plastics and metal, but Kranstenenif—well, Kranstenenif had a different idea."

"What was it?" Alexander asked.

The chairman looked around the room for support, but no one would meet his eye. "Animal parts," he said. "Kranstenenif grafted animal parts onto human beings. I mean—that's what he *wanted* to do. We didn't let him, of course."

"Well, why not?" Alexander said. "I'd rather have a pair of ostrich legs than no legs at all. Wouldn't you, Winterbottom?"

"I couldn't say."

"So what became of this Kranstenenif?"

"Well, after we fired him, he opened up his own laboratory in the Arctic Circle," the chairman said. "No one has heard from him since."

"So even though you didn't know it, Mr. Alexander, you are the single largest property owner inside the Arctic Circle. Your father was smart. He figured what with the Urban Tankmobile helping along global warming and all, the arctic was a good real estate bet, and bought up huge tracts of Canada, Siberia, Norway, Iceland—you name it. Even Greenland. Funny thing about Greenland, it's not very green at all."

Their escort, a realtor named Sven Jurgenson, stopped walking long enough to shrug. "Soon, we hope, but not yet."

Alexander heard a moan from Winterbottom, and looked back to see him struggling with the deep snow and the heavy case he was carrying. The boy smiled at the sight.

"Global warming taking a little longer than he would've liked," Jurgenson continued, "your father had Baddenfield Global Real Estate rent out these properties for whatever they could get. That's how I got stuck—I mean, *assigned*—up here. Anyway, most of our business comes from reindeer herders, loganberry gatherers, evil geniuses, reclusive artists—that sort of thing."

Dr. Kranstenenif, it turned out, had been a Baddenfield tenant for a number of years, having taken over a lab space halfway between the lairs of a hedge fund manager and the writer Thomas Pynchon.

"This used to be all ice, with twenty feet of snow on *top* of the ice," Jurgenson said, making a sweeping gesture at the tundra ahead. "Now look over there: grass! It's only a tuft, but in the middle of the day the ice around it melts into a small pool. It's still cold enough to give you hypothermia like *that*," he went on, snapping his fingers, "but it's a good sign. We'll be selling condos like this was Miami in no time."

"I really think . . . we should reconsider this . . . young

sir," Winterbottom said, huffing and puffing as he caught up. He rested the case on the ground. It was punched through with holes, and if Jurgenson wondered what was inside of it, he figured it better not to ask.

"I mean, a mad scientist? It sounds frightening to me," Winterbottom went on, mopping the sweat from his forehead before it turned to ice.

"Don't be such a wuss," Alexander said, moving on. "C'mon, let's go."

"Well, this is the place," Jurgenson said when they arrived at a giant greenhouse that had been built into the side of a jagged mountain. All the glass, however, was too fogged-up for them to see what was inside.

The agent turned agitated and jittery. He rubbed his hands together and pointed at an intercom beside a rusted iron door. "Well, just go ahead and press that button there—guess I'll be going now," he said, and turned around so fast to leave that he was already gone.

"Do you really think we should just barge in like this?" Winterbottom said. "Unannounced?"

"We tried calling Kranstenenif, but his phone is disconnected," Alexander said peevishly. "What more can we do? He doesn't even have an e-mail address."

Alexander pushed the TALK button on the intercom. A burst of static was followed by a buzz, and the heavy metal door came unlocked.

On the other side of it, they found themselves in a

tropical garden grown out of control. It was partly dying, partly thriving, and so dense you couldn't see more than a few feet ahead. Alexander pushed through the brown fronds of palm bushes and walked around great gnarled masses of prickly pear cactuses, with Winterbottom so close on his heels that he kept tripping.

"Stop that, Winterbottom!"

They came to a clearing near a cave, where the greenhouse met the face of the mountain. "Oh dear," Winterbottom said as Alexander crept closer to the dark mouth of the cave. Before he got there, however, the boy was startled—and Winterbottom positively terrified—by a beast emerging out of the darkness.

But the animal was nothing to be startled by, let alone terrified of. It was a little white pony, and it seemed just as spooked to see Alexander and Winterbottom as vice versa.

The fascinating thing about the animal was that it had a horn coming out of the middle of its forehead. No, wait—the *really* fascinating thing about it was that it had wings!

"A unicorn!" Alexander said, approaching the animal.

The unicorn, raising its head abruptly to Alexander and his outstretched hand, leapt to one side and disappeared into the jungle.

"Wow!" Alexander said.

"Wow!" Alexander said again, this time at a snorting pig. The snort was not coming from a snout, however, but from the trunk of an elephant attached to its face where a snout should have been. The trunk dragged on the ground behind the beast, who walked a little sideways so as not to trip over it.

More Wow!s followed as other animals emerged from the trees and underbrush. There was an aardvark sporting zebra stripes, a donkey hopping on the hindquarters of a kangaroo, bumblebees flapping butterfly wings, and a panda wagging the tail of a dachshund, which even Alexander had to think was cute.

All the mixed-up animals dashed off when they caught sight of Alexander and Winterbottom, except for a hare wearing the shell of a tortoise. It couldn't dash anywhere, being stuck on its back. Its long ears flopped as it thrashed about, while its little cotton tail moved in and out of the back of its shell.

"The poor thing!" Winterbottom said, going to flip the odd little creature onto its belly.

"No, wait—don't!" Alexander said, grabbing Winterbottom by the coat. "It's funny watching it struggle like that!"

"Oh, Alexander Baddenfield, you truly are the worst boy alive," Winterbottom said, tsk-tsking him. "Now let me go!"

"No! I order you *not* to turn that rabbitturtle over!"

"Rabbitturtle? I'd say it's a haretoise. But whatever it is, I'm helping it. Now let go," Winterbottom said, dragging Alexander forward.

"No, stop—I will *fire* you if you turn the rabbitturtle over!"

"*Haretoise*," Winterbottom said, and unplucked Alexander's grip finger by finger.

"Fine," Alexander said, falling to his butt. "Actually, I *order* you to turn it over. I want to see if a rabbitturtle is fast or slow!"

"It is of extremely average speed, actually." The unfamiliar voice came out from the shadows of the cave, followed by a man who walked to where the frustrated beast lay. He flipped it over, and the animal hop-crawled away, neither quickly nor slowly. "And I myself prefer the term 'rabbittortoise.'"

"Ah, rabbit*tortoise*!" Alexander and Winterbottom both said, nodding.

Was this Kranstenenif? He certainly looked mad, if not downright deranged, but not a whole lot like a scientist. His clothes were unkempt, and the closer he came, the more disgusting his personal grooming habits revealed themselves to be. His beard was crumby with specks of food, his rotten-egg breath could wilt a cactus, his ears brimmed with coagulated, cheesy wax, and his red, watery eyes were in a constant state of blink.

Winterbottom looked away so as not to stare, and motioned back toward the cave. "Your unicorn is very beautiful."

Kranstenenif made a harrumphing sound. "Everyone loves the unicorn. The only thing is, I can't make one that flies. Physics! I hate physics! To make a horse fly would take a pair of wings 163.33 feet long. Where can you find a pair of wings like that? Nowhere!" The scientist shook his head at the injustice of it all. "That one you saw has a pair of swan wings on it. Useless."

Suddenly, as if he remembered he was supposed to be angry and annoyed, Kranstenenif gruffly said to his guests, "So! What do you want of the mad Dr. Graft?"

Alexander straightened himself up and said, "I am—"

"I know who you are!" the scientist said. "And if this is about the rent check, let me tell you something, Baddenfield. I've been complaining about the leaky roof in this dump for months, and no one has done a cotton-picking thing about it! Where is that squirrelly real estate agent of yours? Jerkenson. He's been avoiding me forever."

"Whatever you need is yours," Alexander said. "And don't worry about the rent."

"Ah, the famous Baddenfield generosity," the scientist said, his eyes narrowing to a suspicious squint. "What do you want from me in return?"

A cockatoo with the head of a ferret came flying past Alexander's ear. "These mixed-up animals of yours are

cool and all, but what about your other research?" Alexander said. "Combining animals and people?"

"Bah!" Kranstenenif said. "HUMAN research—if only I could!"

"Why can't you?" Alexander said.

"Insurance!" Kranstenenif threw up his arms. "I can't get any insurance!"

"I didn't know mad scientists had to worry about insurance," Winterbottom said.

"*Everybody* has to worry about insurance!"

"Well, that isn't a problem," Alexander sniffed. "Baddenfield Enterprises owns some of the most unscrupulous insurance companies in the world. We'll write you a policy."

"You still haven't told me what you *want*." Kranstenenif squinted his eyes so much, they were now just closed.

"Winterbottom, if you would," Alexander said.

Taking his cue, Winterbottom presented the case he had been lugging all over the Arctic Circle. It was a pet carrier.

"Dr. Kranstenenif, I would like to present Shaddenfrood." Shaddenfrood, unfortunately, was curled up in a ball in the back of the carrier, somewhat ruining the big reveal. Alexander tapped on the case to try to wake him up. *Dumb cat*, he thought. "What I want is for you to remove the nine lives out of this lazy, undeserving creature and transplant them into me."

Kranstenenif stood stonily still. The first movement that came to his body was the fluttering of his right eyelid, like he was about to have a seizure. Or was it a fit of rage? It was neither. The mad scientist began to weep.

"Oh, Alexander Baddenfield, my dear, *dear* boy," Kranstenenif said, throwing his arms around him. No one had ever thrown their arms around him, so Alexander had no idea how to react. "The Fates have sent you here, finally! The quest for Nine Lives is my life's work! My dream. How many years have I sought to do this, and now, *finally*, you have been brought to me." He grabbed the boy by the shoulders and said, "Yes, young Baddenfield! Yes, I will do it. You will have your nine lives!"

"So a cat really *does* have nine lives?" Winterbottom asked skeptically. "The twelve greatest doctors in the world all assured us it's a myth."

"Bah!" Kranstenenif said again. "The twelve greatest ignoramuses, you mean! If one of their club doesn't discover something, they refuse to believe it exists at all! It takes modern science a hundred years to come up with what the common folk have known for a hundred generations! For years modern science said it was barbaric that people used leeches on wounds, but now that some well-paid scientist has 'discovered' they make you heal faster, they have 'medical leeches.'"

"I must say," Alexander said. "I don't care. Not unless it has something to do with me getting my extra nine lives."

"Eight, actually," Kranstenenif said. "A cat has eight extra lives that can be transplanted. But with your one, that makes nine. Let me show you." Kranstenenif reached into the carrier and grabbed Shaddenfrood, who let out an abbreviated and high-pitched *Meow!* "There is a hidden organ unique to cats that I have discovered here, inside the cat's navel."

"The belly button?" Alexander said. "Cats don't have belly buttons!"

"Oh yes they do. They're just covered over with fur. Feel here," Kranstenenif said. "This tiny bump right below the rib cage."

"Cool," Alexander said.

Shaddenfrood purred from all the belly rubbing.

"The extra-life-giving organ inside of it I call the novavivum."

"No-vah-VIH-vum?"

"No-vah-*VEE*-vum," Kranstenenif corrected Alexander. "The novavivum is a reservoir of stem cells left over from the umbilical cord. It communicates with the brain and heart through a bundle of nerves, and when it detects that both have ceased activity and the cat is dead, the novavivum sends a dose of stem cells flowing out to all parts of the body.

Within moments, all injuries heal instantly, whether it's a collapsed lung or a broken leg or a hangnail."

"That's awesome!" Alexander said. "Who knew the unbiblical cord could do that?"

Winterbottom was less enthusiastic. "Excuse my asking, Doctor, but cats break bones all the time, and they take weeks to heal."

"Most true," Kranstenenif said. "Again, it is only when the heart and brain stop *completely* that the novavivum releases its stem cells. So when a cat falls out of a tree and injures its leg, it limps; when it falls out of a thirtieth-story window, it gets up off the pavement and walks away good as new."

"So why eight extra lives, then?" Winterbottom said. "Why not six or ten?"

"Because the novavivum has eight compartments. When the eighth is used up and the ninth life begins, the novavivum shrivels to nothing, which is why no one ever discovered it before." The scientist looked down at Shaddenfrood, who had caught sight of another bumble-fly buzzing around. (Or was it a butterbee?) His tail swished. "The first thing we must do is find out how many of his nine lives our little friend has left."

The cave of the unicorn was the entrance to Dr. Kranstenenif's lab. A flickering fluorescent light exposed a dingy room that seemed to double as Kranstenenif's office and bedroom, with a pillow and a blanket laid out on an old couch. Buckets around the room pinged with drips of water from the ceiling. Unopened bills and notepads full of numbers and odd doodles spilled off his desk, which also had on it a photo of a woman and a young girl.

"Is that your family?" Winterbottom asked.

Kranstenenif picked up the frame and sighed, but said nothing.

The scientist led them through a heavy door that went *whoosh* with the sound of escaping air and then automatically locked tight behind them. Squeezed into a pod, Alexander, Winterbottom, Kranstenenif, and Shaddenfrood were misted from all sides by jets.

"Antibacterializing shower," Kranstenenif said.

How excellent, Winterbottom thought, and made a mental note to get one for back home.

After putting on green medical scrubs and having Winterbottom do the same, Kranstenenif released them from the pod and they entered his laboratory.

The level of hygiene in Kranstenenif's lab was far better than that of his person, giving some small lift to Winterbottom's spirits. His stomach was twisted up into

a tight gnarl, and he wished he had brought his Tums with him, or that at least he could drink a glass of milk. He thought of asking Kranstenenif for one, but feared the milk might come from a crocacow or heiferpotamus or something.

A pair of operating tables stood at the center of the doctor's laboratory. On one was strapped down a monkey, and on the other, an armadillo.

"What were you going to do with them?" Alexander asked.

"It doesn't matter now," Kranstenenif said. He unstrapped the animals and shooed them out.

At the mouth of the cave, the monkey and the armadillo eyed each other. They shared an uncomfortable moment, and then briskly walked their opposite ways.

Back inside, Kranstenenif clipped an X-ray he had taken of Shaddenfrood's torso to a light box.

"Look at this!" Kranstenenif said, and held up a magnifying glass for the others to see. "The entire novavivum— all eight compartments—is entirely intact! I've never seen a more perfect specimen."

"It doesn't surprise me," Alexander said. "The most dangerous thing that cat has ever done is use the litter box."

"So," Kranstenenif said, clapping his hands together. "Let's get this operation going!"

"Right now?" Winterbottom asked.

"Right now," Kranstenenif confirmed.

"Right now!" Alexander agreed.

"But this is so sudden!" Winterbottom said.

"Sudden?" Kranstenenif said. "I've been waiting twenty-five years to do this! It's not sudden at all."

"Yeah, Winterbottom," Alexander said. "And I've been waiting almost a week. Besides, I'm standing around here with just *one* life on my hands. Do you have any idea how risky that is? The sooner I get ahold of those eight extra lives, the better!"

"But-but-but," Winterbottom stammered. "Aren't there tests that need to be done before an operation like this? Some sort of compatibility study between Alexander and the cat?"

"Not really," Kranstenenif said, opening up a case of gleaming stainless-steel surgical instruments.

"Are you sure you know what you're doing?" Winterbottom asked helplessly.

"Well, no one can be *sure* they know what they're doing until they've done it," the doctor said.

"So why haven't you?" Winterbottom asked. "Surely in twenty-five years you found *someone* willing to try the operation."

"Well, the thing that has 'turned off' most people is that to perform the surgery, the patient has to die on the operating table. There's no way to avoid it—the heart has to be disconnected a good ten or fifteen minutes to insert the novavivum."

"And *that* scared people off?" Alexander said. "What's one life to get eight more?"

"But what if you are wrong," Winterbottom said, "and the transplant doesn't work?"

"Well then," Kranstenenif said, "Alexander will be dead for once and for good."

Winterbottom felt as if the floor of the world had just opened up beneath his feet, and generation upon generation of Winterbottoms—all the cautious souls of his ancestors—were calling on him to try and stop this.

You must stop him, Son, the ghost of his father said, tugging at his pants leg. *It is your life's duty!*

"You know, I can't believe that NO ONE was willing to take you up on this!" Alexander said to Kranstenenif.

"To be honest, not that many people believe in me," Kranstenenif said. "I mean, I *am* a mad scientist."

"This is rash," Winterbottom said, summoning a strength he had never before possessed. "The rashest of all rash things that have ever been done, and it is up to me to stop you! Do you know that when Nikolas Boddenveld ate that tulip bulb, there was a Winderboddem saying, *I don't think that's an onion, sir!* And when Pieter Boddenveld tried to buy Canada for a dollar fifty's worth of trinkets, his Winderboddem told him, *I don't think these Indians will fall for it, sir!* Alexander, you are the last of the Baddenfields, and it is up to you to carry on the family traditions, but please end this one tradition of

not listening to a Winterbottom when he is about to save your life! For this quack will surely take it." Winterbottom turned to Kranstenenif. "No offense."

It was a rousing speech. Even Kranstenenif, who well should have been offended by it, was not. He was very nearly moved.

And Alexander? Neither very, nor nearly, nor moved at all.

"Oh, save all that historical hooey for someone who cares, Winterbottom," the boy said. "What is the absolute worst thing that could happen if this operation doesn't work?"

"You will die."

"Exactly," Alexander said. "Which we all know is going to happen anyway—at a young age, in some weird and crazy way. The Baddenfield way. If the operation fails, I'll just be following in the footsteps of my ancestors. If it succeeds, you should be the happiest person alive, because I'll have nine times as many lives to end."

Winterbottom, still so taken with his own words, couldn't find the ones with which to respond to Alexander's.

"Here," Kranstenenif said, wheeling a tray of surgical implements over to Winterbottom.

"What are you giving me these for?" Winterbottom said.

"You're going to be my assistant."

"Oh, no," Winterbottom said. "I may not be able to make Alexander's decisions for him, but I can make them for myself, and I absolutely refuse to be a party to this."

"Well, it'll be a lot more risky if I have to do this alone," Kranstenenif said, scratching his head. "But okay."

The scientist began shaving Shaddenfrood's belly where he would have to make the first incision.

"And you, Alexander," Winterbottom said. "Are you okay with it being risky?"

"Absolutely," the boy said.

Say what you will about Alexander Baddenfield: He was rude, he was mean, he was a brat. But the boy was fearless. Winterbottom wasn't sure why his ancestors had so loyally served the Baddenfields down through the generations, but he knew why he himself did.

Defeated, dejected, Winterbottom turned to the mad scientist and said, "Tell me what to do."

Even Alexander Baddenfield, for all his bravado, had a moment of doubt looking into the flaring green eyes of Dr. Kranstenenif as the scientist reached down to administer the anesthetic. The boy could feel his hot, stinking breath, and see the sesame seeds in his beard. Alexander felt the slightest twinge of nerves, but it was too late. The anesthetic took effect, and Alexander no longer cared, not about a single thing in the world. He saw the operation unfold over him in slow motion, saw

Dr. Kranstenenif's face tie up in knots of concentration while he worked, saw Winterbottom look sicker and sicker with worry. Alexander loved making Winterbottom worry. It was funny. If only he could laugh.

Then, something not so funny happened. Alexander felt a coldness inside of his chest, as if long chilly fingers were taking hold of his heart. As unpleasant as that feeling was, Alexander missed it when it was replaced by a sort of bloated numbness that spread out across his entire body. And then, Alexander felt nothing at all.

At 2:54 p.m. on Thursday, the 17th of August, Alexander Baddenfield, the last of the Baddenfields, expired at the age of twelve.

The operation was a complete success.

Warning
to
ALL READERS

Yｏu are about to embark on a tale that recounts the sometimes gruesome deaths of a young boy, and his not always pleasant rebirths. If you are squeamish, sentimental, or faint of heart, I suggest that you turn back now. You have hopefully enjoyed the story so far. Why not quit while you are ahead?

If you are made of sterner stuff, however, and decide to continue, I present to you . . .

The Second Life
of
ALEXANDER BADDENFIELD

*T*ick, *tick, tick* went his father's old pocket watch, or at least Winterbottom imagined that's what he heard as the seconds and minutes passed after Alexander's death. Winterbottom's palms dripped with nervous sweat, and he had to keep wiping off the surgical instruments before he handed them to the doctor. *Tick, tick, tick*, and still the line on the heart monitor stayed flat. How long could this go on before it was too late to bring Alexander back?

"How long is too long, Doctor?"

"Well, this is weird," Kranstenenif said, ruffling his brow as he peered into Alexander's open chest. "I didn't expect to see that!"

"What is it?" Winterbottom asked, and felt pain in his own chest. "Didn't expect to see what?"

He begged the scientist for more information, but

Kranstenenif just said, "Nothing, nothing," and kept glancing over at an anatomy book he had left propped open for reference.

Alexander laughed at Winterbottom. Well, he couldn't really laugh, just like he couldn't exactly feel anything, or hear. Yet he did somehow understand what Winterbottom and the doc were saying—what they were thinking, even. *Being dead is cool!* Alexander thought. He just kind of floated above the room, watching everything, himself included. It was funny; he didn't quite look like he thought he did. There was a big difference between seeing yourself in a mirror or a photo and *actually* seeing yourself. He could even see his insides, guts and all. Once Dr. Kranstenenif began to sew him up, Alexander was extra glad to be dead—that needle looked like it hurt.

Yes, being dead was cool, but then something *not* cool happened.

Alexander suddenly felt wretched, like he needed to vomit. The main difference, of course, was that he was back to feeling anything at all. And he was no longer floating above the room—everything had gone to black. Flashes of light came to Alexander, as his consciousness turned over like an ignition: *spark, spark, spark,* **FIRE**. With that, his nervous system switched on like a hydrant turned to full blast, but with no one to hold the hose. All the pain hit him at once—every cut, every stitch. His heart took its first big pound painfully against his

rib cage, and Alexander gasped in his first new breath of air—HUHNGH!—which hit the walls of his dormant lungs like lemon juice on chapped lips.

Next thing he knew, he was getting up from the operating table, his mouth open in the middle of an uncontrollable, face-splitting yawn. He opened his eyes. The pain—where had it gone?

"How do you feel?" Winterbottom asked nervously.

"I feel like . . . I feel . . . " Alexander said. "I don't know the word for how I feel." He looked down at his chest, which had looked like Frankenstein's neck a minute ago but was now as smooth as it was the day he was born. "Where's the scar?"

"No scar," Dr. Kranstenenif said. "You are on your second life now. You're good as new."

"Good as new?" Winterbottom said.

"That's the word," Alexander said. "*New*. That's how I feel—new!"

"So the operation actually worked?" Winterbottom said.

"It worked," the doctor said with a grin.

"It worked!" Alexander said, jumping off the table.

"It worked, it worked, it worked!" the three of them chanted, hugging each other. After one too many hugs for his liking, Alexander left Winterbottom and Kranstenenif to do the embracing and started putting on his clothes.

"Okay, guys," he said when he was done. "I'm outta here."

"But I need to hold you for observation!" Kranstenenif said. "I need to run tests!"

"That sounds boring," Alexander said. "I hate tests. That's why I quit school. Besides, I've never felt better in my whole life." Alexander grabbed Shaddenfrood off the operating table and put him into the carrier. The cat woke up, saw the bald patch on his tummy, gave it a few licks, and went back to sleep.

"What I need to do is go try on my new lives for size," Alexander said, pressing the button of the exit door, which opened *whoosh*. "I won't feel comfortable until I've used up at least two or three of them."

That last comment erased all the relief and joy from Winterbottom's heart. "Please, Alexander," he said, following him out of the lab. "Listen to what the doctor is saying!"

"Alexander! You must understand, you are not invincible!" Kranstenenif called after him through the thick jungle of the greenhouse. "There are rules to this! There are still ways you can die for good! Even a vampire dies if you put a stake through his heart!"

"Wait," Alexander said, stopping before he opened the door to the arctic deep-freeze. "Are you saying I'm a vampire?"

"Well, no," Kranstenenif said, disappointing Alexan-

der. "But if someone drove a stake through your heart, and you couldn't get it out, you would keep dying, coming back to life, and dying again, until all your lives were used up."

"Okay, got it," Alexander said, and walked away into the snow back toward the plane.

"Wait, there's more!" Kranstenenif said, but Alexander was too far away.

"You'd better tell me instead, Doctor," Winterbottom said. "It's not like Alexander will listen anyway."

Kranstenenif went through how broken bones, cracked ribs, concussions, and the like wouldn't heal any differently from before, not unless Alexander died and came back to life. Even more important, a lost arm or leg would never grow back. "And if the kid loses his head," Kranstenenif said, "it's Humpty Dumpty time."

"Meaning?"

"He can never be put back together again."

Winterbottom hurried away from the mad scientist's lair and quickly spotted Alexander stopping not too far ahead. He was taking his clothes off.

"Alexander! What on earth are you doing?"

"Going for a swim!" Alexander said, standing on the patch of grass Jurgenson had pointed out earlier. A pool of melted ice had indeed formed around it. "That real estate guy said this would kill a person real quick! Hypodermics!"

"Hypothermia, Alexander."

"Whatever," he said. "Now take out your pocket watch and time how quick I die!"

"I will not!" Winterbottom said, crossing his arms. "Alexander Baddenfield, put your clothes back on this instant. I demand it!"

Not listening, the boy dipped in a toe, and quickly yanked it back out. The water was more than cold—it burned. The tip of Alexander's big toe turned purple, and a breeze blew a dusting of snow onto his naked back.

"I think I want to find a warmer way to die first," Alexander said, and started putting his clothes back on.

Down below, the clouds looked like a soft, feathery mattress. Soft, but solid. Could it really be true that a person would fall right through them? It didn't seem like it. It seemed like you could lie down on top of them and go to sleep.

"Winterbottom," Alexander said, shaking him. "Have them open the door of the plane. I'm gonna jump!"

"Really, Alexander, can't you at least wait until we get home to die again?" Winterbottom said, not bothering to lift the eye mask covering half of his face. "Besides, I don't share your death wish, nor, I'm sure, do the

pilot or flight attendant, who would also be sucked out if we opened the door midflight." He then warned Alexander again about Humpty Dumpty time. "From this high up you'd crack into a thousand pieces and be dead for good."

Back in New York, Alexander's driver, Sam, picked them up at the airport. Sam was shaped like an old cigar butt, the same height as Alexander but four times as thick. As always, he opened the back door for Alexander, so he could get into his booster seat.

"Oh no," the boy said, shaking his head. "From now on, Alexander Baddenfield rides in the front seat."

Winterbottom took a deep breath, while Sam just shrugged and did what he was told.

"So this is what the car looks like from up here," Alexander said, climbing in. "Cool." He ran a hand along the dashboard and messed with the radio.

"Now if you'll just put on your seat belt, boss kid, I'll take you home," Sam said, clicking his own into place.

"Seat belt?" Alexander said. "I ain't wearin' no seat belt."

Winterbottom gasped. "No *seat belt*!"

"Why should I wear a seat belt? I'm not in the same boat as you two suckers," Alexander said, and put his feet out the window. "I've got lives to spare. One life! *Hah!* Good luck with that!"

"Whatever you say, boss kid," Sam said, and put the car into drive.

"You really should buckle your seat belt, sir," Winterbottom said.

One Mississippi, two Mississippi, three Mississippi.

"You really should buckle your seat belt, sir."

One Mississippi, two Mississippi, three Mississippi.

"You really should buckle your seat belt, sir."

One Mississippi, two Mississippi, three Mississippi.

"You really should buckle your seat belt, sir."

One Mississippi, two Mississippi, three Mississippi.

"You really should—"

"Shut *up*, Winterbottom."

Winterbottom bit his lip.

One Mississippi, two Mississippi, three Mississippi, four *Mississippi*, **five** *Mississippi*, **SIX** *Mississippi*, ***SEVEN***—

"You really should buckle your seat belt, sir."

Turning off Canal Street at the corner of Bouwerie Lane, Sam parked in a spot opposite Baddenfield Castle. Alexander hopped out of the car and, without looking, walked right across the middle of the street.

"Alexander!" Winterbottom yelled. "Watch where you are going!"

And he really should have.

Jean-Luc-Pierre Toussaint, a taxi cab driver from Haiti— or more lately, Queens—had just dropped off his final

fare of the evening. As he pulled away from the curb he glanced down to flick the switch for his OFF DUTY light. Looking back up he saw—A BOY!

Swerving, he narrowly missed the child—WHAT WAS HE DOING IN THE MIDDLE OF THE STREET!—and nearly hit a Prius in the right lane. Swerving back the other way, he ran his cab up onto the sidewalk and almost hit a fire hydrant.

"YOU CRAZY CHILD!" Jean-Luc-Pierre shook his fist out the window at the boy. "LEARN HOW TO CROSS THE STREET! AND YOU," he said to the young man, grabbing him, "TAKE BETTER CONTROL OF YOUR LITTLE BROTHER!"

"I'm sorry, I'm sorry!" the older one yelled back.

These people! Jean-Luc-Pierre thought to himself. Typical New Yorkers . . .

Winterbottom watched the cabdriver screech away still shaking a fist and honking. He turned to Alexander. "What were you *thinking*? How many times have we gone over this? Look left, look right, look left again, *then* cross."

"Like I told you," Alexander said, "I don't have to worry about this stuff anymore. At least not until I'm down to three lives or so." Alexander pressed the code on the buzzer, and with clanks and a steady hum the

drawbridge lowered. At the base of it, a rat missing half its tail jumped down into the moat and swam away.

"Alexander, the world cannot function if one person is so utterly reckless," Winterbottom said. "It would be chaos!"

Before the drawbridge even touched the sidewalk, Alexander hopped onto it and ran into Baddenfield Castle. With a sigh, Winterbottom trudged across the planks. Then he thought, *Maybe I should be running too.*

Up in the kitchen, he found Alexander on a step-ladder rifling through Winterbottom's personal cabinet of food. "Alexander—what are you doing? That's my food! How did you find the key?"

"Top of the cabinet," Alexander said. "Real tricky, Winterbottom."

"What are you looking for in there?" he said nervously, trying to peer over Alexander's shoulder.

"The most forbidden fruit of all," the boy said, and found what he was looking for. "Peanut butter!"

"But Alexander, you don't want to eat that. Allergies are so—"

"And white bread . . ." Alexander said, pulling a bag from the shelf. "And bananas!" He hopped down, got out the silverware, and began making a sandwich.

"Put . . . the knife . . . down . . ." Winterbottom said. "Please."

"Don't be so worried all the time," Alexander said,

taking a bite. "I mean, what are the chances I'm allergic to this stuff? One in a million?"

But as he chewed, the boy's smile turned flat. His brows knotted, and he grabbed his throat. *"Hnnh!"*

"What is it?" Winterbottom said, alarmed.

"Hnnh!" the boy went again, heaving.

"Are you all right? Alexander! Can you breathe?"

"Hnnh!"

"Oh no. Oh no!"

"Hnnh!" Alexander's face turned purple and his eyes bulged.

"Must call Dr. Sorrow . . ." Winterbottom said, fumbling for his phone.

"Ah-ha-ha!" Alexander cackled. "Gotcha!" In three more bites he finished downing one half of the sandwich and smacked his lips. "Now where do you keep the milk?"

For the first three days of his second life, Alexander did all the things that he had been told never to do but couldn't see a good reason for not doing. Winterbottom kept all such activities on itemized lists, which made the task easy.

First came the food. Alexander embarked on one of the most disgusting eating binges in history, combining all the items—nuts, milk, cheese, ice cream, bread,

pasta, soy, shellfish, eggs, and onions—that had previously been off-limits, and which led him to discover that he didn't have a single allergy. He ate genetically modified *everything*, but even that wasn't enough. Alexander wanted to test other kinds of foods—dangerous foods. The kinds that could kill you right away. Like washing down a roll of Mentos with a can of Coke.

As it wound up, you didn't die from that—it was an urban legend. But it did give you a really bad stomachache, which, from Alexander's perspective, was worse.

Alexander also gave up on most basic precautions. Beyond ignoring all car safety and pedestrian rules, he no longer washed his hands before eating, brushed his teeth, or flossed. He went outside without any sunblock on, and even took escalators with untied shoelaces.

Another of Winterbottom's lists named all the pets that Alexander had asked for but Winterbottom had refused to get. Included were tarantulas, scorpions, piranhas, and the most dangerous house pet in the world: the python.

"I call him . . . *Cortez*!" Alexander said. "Most people only get the little two- or three-foot pythons, but Cortez is ten feet long and then some. That's *way* big enough to kill a dog. Or a goat, I think."

"Really, Alexander, isn't a cat enough of a pet to have?" Winterbottom said.

"Aren't you the one who's always worried that the rats

in the moat are carrying the plague? Well, pythons eat rats." And with that, Alexander pulled a rat he had spent most of the morning trapping out of a bag, and proudly dropped it into Cortez's glass terrarium.

The canal rat, the one missing a chunk of its tail, scurried into a corner and stared at the python. The rat's chest beat up and down.

"Do you see how scared it is? Go for the kill, Cortez! Kill, kill!"

"Alexander, this is appalling."

Except that it wasn't. The python cocked its head slightly to look at the rodent, blinked, and then rested its head back down.

"What's wrong with you, snake?" Alexander said, tapping the glass.

Small victories can be the best kind, thought Winterbottom.

One last major item remained on Winterbottom's safety precaution list. This one had particularly to do with New York, and Alexander was convinced it too must be an urban legend: that touching the third rail would kill you.

"But it *will* kill you!"

"Why should I listen to you?" Alexander said to Winterbottom. "You're the one who put Mentos and Coke on

the death list. Besides, it's common sense. Do you really think they would leave the third rail out there for people to touch if you could die from it? A shock, maybe, but electrocution? That's crazy!"

"But the third rail is how subway trains get power," Winterbottom said. "And nobody touches it, because everybody *knows* not to."

Haplessly, Winterbottom argued with Alexander all the way down the stairs, over the drawbridge, onto the sidewalk, and down to the corner subway station. On the tracks, a Z train was pulling out of the station, so the platform was empty except for a man who had missed his train and was now shaking his head. He happened to be wearing a top hat.

"When you're down to your last life and you're wishing you had this one back," Winterbottom said as Alexander climbed down to the track bed, "just remember who told you so."

"Hey, kid! What are you doing down there?" the man who had missed the train yelled. "You demented or something?"

"No," Alexander said, "I'm just trying to see whether or not the third rail will electrocute me." Alexander stepped over the first rail, knelt down on the second, and poised himself above the third. "Okay, here goes!" he said, and latched both hands onto the top of it, ready for a mind-blowing jolt.

Nothing happened.

"See, Winterbottom?" Alexander said. "I told you it was just a myth."

"Thank goodness."

"Hey, kid," the man waiting for the train said. "That's just the protective cover. You gotta grab underneath it if you really wanna check."

"Oh," Alexander said. "Thanks!"

The Third Life
of
ALEXANDER BADDENFIELD

This time, it was like a light switch being turned off and then back on. Alexander wasn't even sure what had happened to him, until he noticed that his clothes were black and smoking and his hair was standing straight on end.

"I guess they weren't kidding about *that* one, were they!" Alexander said. "That was mad cool! How can I die next?"

Just then, a light appeared in the tunnel, and it became very clear how Alexander could die next. Before he could think to move, however, Winterbottom was down on the tracks, pushing him back up onto the platform. Winterbottom only managed not getting hit by the train himself because Alexander and the top-hatted man each grabbed one of his arms and hauled him up out of the way.

"Winterbottom, what are you doing? You could have killed yourself trying to save me!" Alexander shook his head. "You need to be more careful."

The next morning, Alexander considered ways to begin—and potentially end—his new life.

"Haven't you done enough dying for one week? At this rate, that rodent is going to outlive you," Winterbottom said, nodding over to the glass home of Cortez. The canal rat had taken to sleeping in the big python's coils and was happily enjoying several meals a day, while Cortez had yet to do anything but take sips of water and lie about.

"Well, it doesn't have to be something that will kill me," Alexander said. "At least, not for sure. But it has to be dangerous. And fun."

"Well," Winterbottom said, thinking. "Maybe you should go running *very* fast . . . in your bare feet . . . until you are all out of breath! Now wouldn't *that* be fun?"

"What would you know about fun, Winterbottom?"

Alexander looked out the window and saw three kids on skateboards. One of them stopped and stomped his foot down on the back of his board, flipping it into his hand. He tucked it under his arm, waved good-bye to his friends, and went into the subway.

"On the other hand, Winterbottom, maybe something sporty is exactly what I need."

Cooped up in his castle all those years for his own protection, Alexander had never done a single outdoor activity. To discourage the idea, Winterbottom would attach to the refrigerator every awful sports injury, hiking accident, and getting-lost-at-sea story he could find. He wouldn't even allow the boy to learn to swim, for fear he would drown practicing.

Of Alexander's attempts at skateboarding, the less said the better. He quickly perfected the stomp, flip, and tuck move, and then decided he was ready for the half-pipe. He and Winterbottom went to the skatepark on Pier 62, and Alexander's attempts on the ramps might well have snuffed out his third life, but instead just led to scrapes, bruises, and a possible concussion. It ended with the boy hurling his brand-new skateboard into the river.

Next, Alexander decided to try biking, which went no better until Winterbottom convinced the boy to get training wheels. Alexander began to have fun, and even be a little proud of himself, until a seven-year-old girl on a pink bike passed him like he was standing still. "Ha ha, big baby!" she said, turning around and

laughing. "Nice training wheels, dude!" The bike soon followed the skateboard into the Hudson. And then so did Alexander.

Walking down to the marina, Alexander bought a kayak. Water seemed softer than concrete, and paddling looked easier than biking. Alexander figured he'd do a quick loop around Manhattan, and maybe make a detour to see the Statue of Liberty. He got into his new boat.

"Here's your life jacket," the guy who sold him the kayak said, holding up a bright orange vest.

"Save it for the road crews," Alexander said, pushing away from the dock with his oar.

Winterbottom had by now realized that the time for more drastic measures had arrived. While Alexander was purchasing his kayak, Winterbottom had rented a motorboat to follow the boy. With Sam the driver steering, Winterbottom opened the app on his phone that showed Alexander's exact location, thanks to a tracking chip he'd implanted in the boy years before.

Alexander quickly realized that this whole kayaking thing was a lot less fun than it looked. For one thing, it took a lot of work to paddle oneself forward. What was worse, just when Alexander had finally worked up some speed, his boat got hit by the wake of a garbage scow, nearly knocking him over. Spitting out a mouthful of grayish-brown harbor water, he found himself pushed back to practically where he had started.

"Have you had enough yet?" Winterbottom yelled through a bullhorn.

"No, this is great! So much fun!" Alexander shouted, even though it was getting less fun by the minute. His arms were now burning and so was his face—maybe sunblock wasn't such a bad idea. What was worse, he couldn't figure out how to steer the thing. It seemed to be going in the opposite direction of where he wanted to go, which was away from a water taxi that was closing in on him. The faster and harder Alexander paddled, the more his lungs began to burn, and then a pain stabbed him in the ribs. He was unsure whether he was having a heart attack or whether this was just what exercise felt like. Either way, he didn't like it.

Alexander narrowly missed the nose of the water taxi, but went tumbling all the same, caught in its rippling wake. Thrown from the kayak, Alexander went plummeting into the sea, sucking down salt water that stung the back of his throat, went up his nose, and set fire to every nick and scrape on his elbows and knees, not to mention his sunburned face. He struggled for a while, and then he struggled no more.

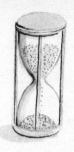

The Fourth Life
of
ALEXANDER BADDENFIELD

ut off by the water taxi, Winterbottom lost sight of Alexander for a moment. After the boxy yellow boat passed, all he could see was the overturned kayak. Winterbottom congratulated himself on his tracking chip as he located the boy on his phone's screen and directed Sam to where Alexander was.

"There he is!" Sam the driver yelled, and Winterbottom—a certified lifeguard—dove into the water and dragged the boy into the boat.

"How long does it take for him to come back to life?" Sam asked as he turned the boat around and sped for the docks.

"I'm not sure he's dead. I think he just passed out," Winterbottom said, and started delivering CPR to Alexander.

Oops. Better make that . . .

The Third Life
of
ALEXANDER BADDENFIELD,
CONT'D

Alexander woke up coughing and spitting out water.

"Drowning is a *horrible* way to die," Alexander said, still gagging as Sam pulled the boat into the marina. "No more water sports."

"Thank goodness," Winterbottom said, and helped a woozy Alexander up onto the wet dock while Sam tied the boat to a cleat. "Now, Alexander, perhaps you will learn to enjoy and not waste all that has been given to you. As my father always said, it is the careful man who pays attention to the world around him who succeeds in—"

Winterbottom never got to his point—or his father's—as the next sound out of his mouth was a cry of pain. He had slipped stepping onto the dock, his leg going in one direction, and his foot the other.

"It's not too bad, Winterbottom. A mild sprain. Keep this tape around it for a week and don't put too much pressure on it, and the ankle should be fine."

"Thank you, Dr. Sorrow," Winterbottom said.

Alexander had spent all of Dr. Sorrow's visit in a surly mood, twisted up in a bearskin blanket, his back to the physician and his red-skinned face toward the flames of Baddenfield Castle's walk-in fireplace. He surely needed medical attention himself, but Alexander wouldn't give Dr. Sorrow the satisfaction. Instead, he decided to chide the doctor.

"I bet you feel pretty stupid now, Mr. First-Best Doctor in the World."

"And why would I feel stupid?" Dr. Sorrow said, packing up his bag.

"You said there was no such thing as a cat having nine lives, and yet they do, and now so do I."

"How are you so certain you have these nine lives?"

"I've already used up two of them," Alexander said, crossing his arms. "Yes, I know what dying is all about, and being alive too. More than you'll ever know."

"Tell me, Alexander," Dr. Sorrow said. "Have you ever heard the story of Icarus?"

Alexander shrugged.

"Icarus had a father named Daedalus who created a pair of wings out of feathers and wax. Daedalus told the boy to fly neither too high to the sun nor too low to the sea, because both were dangerous. Rather, he should stick to the middle course where it was safe. Icarus didn't listen to his father, and was having such a good time that he decided to fly all the way up to the sun. But the sun melted the wax, and one by one the feathers fell from his wings until Icarus was left flapping his bare arms. He fell into the sea and drowned, never to fly—or live—again."

"That's a great story," Alexander said, sitting up. "Winterbottom, I need a set of wings like that!"

Dr. Sorrow sighed, stood up, and shook his head walking out. He should have known better.

The Icarus idea brought a pleasing period of safe activity to Baddenfield Castle, at least as far as Winterbottom was concerned. Alexander was so taken with the idea of flying that he forgot about the idea of dying. He even lost interest in his menagerie of poisonous and murderous pets, no longer bothered by his python's conspicuous lack of appetite. In fact, Winterbottom had never seen Alexander so absorbed in anything before, and even dared hope that this whole crazy adventure would turn

out for the best. Until, that is, the wings were finished and Winterbottom found himself standing on the 86th-floor observation deck of the Empire State Building.

Of feathers and wax these wings were not. The aerodynamics experts and computer engineers at Baddenfield Aeronautics had created a technological masterpiece for Alexander, a pair of self-correcting, heat-proof glider wings. Daedalus could have done no better.

"These wings are not only aerodynamically but ergonomically perfect," the technician strapping in Alexander explained. "Flying with these is as simple as flapping your arms. Keep your palms flat inside the wings to maintain present altitude, rotate them thumbs up to go higher, and thumbs down to descend. The computer chips stitched into the fabric will take care of the rest."

"See, Winterbottom. This isn't dangerous at all."

"Do you even know what 'ergonomically' means, Alexander?"

"Of course I do," Alexander said, getting ready to jump. "It means 'birdlike.'"

With that, Alexander took a big breath and started to run for the railing at the edge of the deck. Immediately, the wings lifted him up and over the heads of the Baddenfield personnel and tourists crowding the 86th-floor porch. The controls for the wings were so natural, he hardly had to think about them, and almost immedi-

ately Alexander was diving and swooping and doing a circle around the spire of the Empire State Building, to the cheers of the people watching below.

But it wasn't just those on the observation deck who noticed Alexander. As he flew through the canyons of midtown, people on their balconies and in their offices looked agog at the flying boy. For the first time in his life Alexander had fond, warm thoughts of his fellow man, the little people who now crowded Broadway to aim their cameras and cell phones skyward to capture a photo of him. Ah yes, the little people—getting littler the higher he soared. Alexander found himself simultaneously charged with a surge of adrenaline and soothed by the quiet peace of the sky.

In spite of the tale of Icarus—or because of it—Alexander found himself overwhelmed by the urge to get nearer to the sun. Alexander flapped his wings harder and harder, flying up to touch the clouds and to go through them. They weren't solid after all! His face went moist, and he got a bit cold. And it was then, when he had almost reached the heavens, that Alexander came undone. But not by the sun. It was on account of an itch.

His arms had gotten completely, indescribably, irresistibly *itchy*. It was one of those can't-live-without-scratching-it kind of itches. What were these wings made of? Winterbottom had always insisted on Alex-

ander wearing nothing but organic cotton clothing, but these were some kind of plastic he must have been allergic to. He knew he shouldn't do it, but finally Alexander couldn't resist—he *had* to scratch. Moving one arm across the other, however, ruined the aerodynamic balance of the wings, and Alexander suddenly began to drop, then spiral. The wings wrapped around him like a cocoon, and as his plummet turned into a free fall, his skin felt like it would rip off his face. Alexander gasped for breath. He then remembered what Winterbottom had told him in the plane about Humpty Dumpty. If he hit the pavement from so high up, he'd never survive.

His head had begun to go faint, but with his last ounce of strength Alexander spread apart his fingers. He began to spin the other way, and his wings unspooled at the same time he found himself hurtling down the side of the Empire State Building, past floor 102 . . .

101

100

99

98

97

96

95

94

93

92

91

90

89

88

87

86

85

84

83

82

81

80

79

78

77

76

75

74

73

72

71

70

69

68

67

66

65

64

63

62

61

60

59

58

57

56

55

54

53

52

51

50

49

48

47

46

45

44

43

42

41

40

39

3—

Then, like an umbrella popping open, the wings caught air and jerked him back aloft. After a quiet drift upward, he came to a perfect soft landing at the very spot on the 86th-floor observation deck from which he had taken off.

Bravos and clapping surrounded him. What a glorious day for Alexander! What Baddenfield had ever anywhere had people *cheer* for him? Even Winterbottom, quite in spite of himself, had to applaud.

It was like he was traveling through a dream.

In the car on the way home, Alexander replayed every detail of the day in his mind. For the first time since he was born, he felt truly alive. People said that kind of stupid crap all the time, but they didn't know the half of it. If you went around worried about the one life you might lose, then you were as good as dead already. It paid to be reckless. In fact—

Alexander's train of thought was interrupted by the sight of a black cat in the middle of the street. Alexander and the cat met eye to eye. They stared at each other for what seemed like a while but could only have been a split second. Sam the driver swerved and smashed into an oncoming car, and Alexander Baddenfield was ejected from his unstrapped-in perch on the front seat. The boy went crashing through the windshield, was sent hurtling across the street, and smashed skull-first into a brick wall.

By the time his body fell to the sidewalk, Alexander was already dead.

The Fourth Life
of
ALEXANDER BADDENFIELD
(For Real This Time)

Winterbottom and Sam reached Alexander just as he began his new life. His face and clothes covered with blood, Alexander looked like a horror, and behaved like one too.

"Why didn't you just run that stupid cat over!" he said to Sam. "It probably has lots of lives left!"

"And you have fewer and fewer," Winterbottom said.

Alexander remained undaunted.

"Oh, who's counting? Besides, I can always just get another cat and tack on eight more lives, can't I?" He wiped the blood away from his forehead, which was completely smooth. "In fact, we should use *that* cat," he said, nodding in the direction of where the black one had run off. "He owes me one."

Yes, there is no daunt in the boy, Winterbottom thought.

By any standards, it was an utterly, completely ridiculous sight. "Alexander," Winterbottom said, "what are you doing in that old Halloween costume?"

"This is no costume. This was the outfit worn by Pedro Romero Martínez, the greatest bullfighter of all time, when his portrait was painted by Goyá," Alexander said, turning to admire himself in the mirror. "That's the bean guy."

Winterbottom wasn't sure what to make fun of first. The sequins? The purple short pants and matching jacket? The ruffled shirt? The turquoise sash? No, the hat. "It makes you look like a Mouseketeer."

Alexander ignored him. He waved his red cape back and forth in front of Shaddenfrood and shouted, "*Olé! Olé*, you dumb cat."

"Dare I ask what this is leading to?"

"We leave tonight for Pamplona," Alexander said. "That's in Spain. Tomorrow afternoon, I will be the third and final matador in the bullring at Plaza de Toros."

Bullfighting. So this is what it had come to. Winterbottom didn't have the strength to argue. He supposed every Winterbottom had gone through the same thing, in one way or the other.

"I'll start packing," Winterbottom said.

"Excellent! And when you're done, pack for me too. *Olé!*" he said, and twirled around, his red cape fluttering above his head. "I have to practice."

Alexander cranked the handle on his great-great-grandfather's old record player and put on a *paso doble* from an album called *Songs of the Torero*. Facing himself in the mirror, Alexander cocked his hat down over his forehead, picked up his *estoque*—that's a matador's sword—and started stabbing imaginary bulls to the *DUNT dadaDUNT dadaDUNT dadaDUNT-DUNT* of the music. "Take that! *Olé!* And that! *Olé!* And that!"

In the mirror, Alexander couldn't take his eyes off of himself, he looked so magnificent in that hat. He felt Shaddenfrood rub against his leg. But it seemed longer than Shaddenfrood—and then it crossed up over his thighs. He looked down.

"Cortez?"

Before he could do a single other thing, the python wrapped itself around Alexander's chest, pinning his arms to his sides, and started curling around his neck.

Cortez, roused from his sleep by the music, had seen Alexander from behind, wearing the hat, and thought it was the biggest mouse he had ever seen. And since it had been three weeks since the pet store owner had fed him, it was time for his next meal.

"*Now . . . you're . . . hungry . . .*" Alexander said, his voice getting strangled out of him.

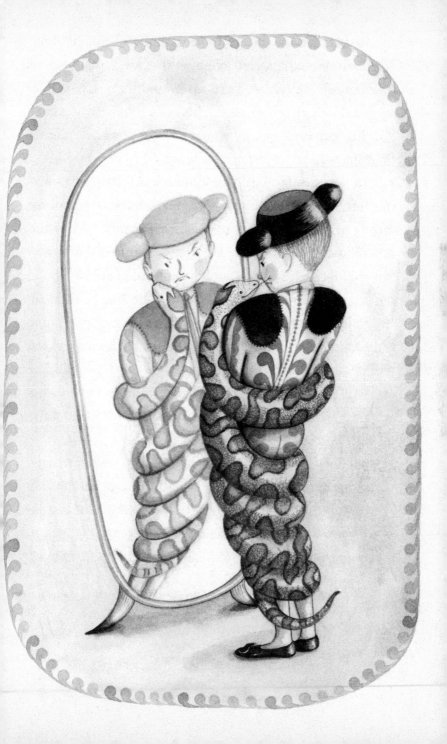

He still had the *estoque* in his right hand, and he managed to place the sharp point of it against the neck of the python. He pressed the tip in and then—*Sssss!*—the snake flinched and squeezed his coils tighter. Alexander lost his grip on the handle, and the sword went clanging to the ground.

The only body part he could still move—barely—was his left hand. He managed to slip it into the front pocket of the great Pedro Romero Martínez's pants and switch his phone on. He then began to press around the screen for the DIAL icon. When he hit the right spot, the phone automatically called the last person he had spoken to. By that time, however, Alexander was feeling the now familiar chilly fingers of death on his heart, and passed out.

Winterbottom was just sticking his underwear in his suitcase when his phone started ringing. ALEXANDER the screen said.

"Hello?" he said. "Hello, Alexander?" He heard rustling. Pocket dialing. The boy was always pocket dialing. Winterbottom knew the sound all too well. But did he also hear . . . the *paso doble?*

Winterbottom shook his head, and pressed END on his phone.

The Fifth Life
of
ALEXANDER BADDENFIELD

As soon as he hung up the phone, Winterbottom had a vision of doom, and the urge to run downstairs to make sure Alexander was all right. But then Alexander would make fun of him, because that's what Alexander always did. And maybe he was right to do it. It was true that Winterbottom was a nervous nellie—he had to admit it—and to what end, now that Alexander had so many extra lives? He went back to packing his underwear.

Then he stopped. He couldn't change even if he wanted to. Winterbottom let the underwear drop and hurried up the stairs to Alexander's room.

DUNT dadaDUNT dadaDUNT dadaDUNT-DUNT, the music went—but no sign of Alexander. Just his awful new pets and, of course, Shaddenfrood. Now where could Alexander have gone? He took out his phone and called him.

Ever so faintly, Winterbottom heard the ring of Alexander's phone. Had he left it in the room? It sounded like it was under the bed, maybe. He searched around. That was when he noticed something different about the python—it looked like it had just eaten an elephant. Whatever was inside of the snake moved. The phone stopped ringing.

"Winnerboddommmmm!" came a muffled voice on the other end of the line. *"Lemme oudda here!"*

"Alexander!" Winterbottom said. "My goodness! Hang on! I'll get the syrup of ipecac!"

"Whad?"

"Never mind!" Winterbottom said, running. "You'll see what it is!"

When he returned, Winterbottom had a moment of pause before getting too close to the snake. But the python appeared to be either catatonic from its enormous meal or incredibly ill. Either way, the beast gave him little resistance when he lifted up its head, spread its jaws, and poured the whole bottle of ipecac down its gullet.

The eyes of the python went wide, it began to gag and heave, and then—in one generous hurl—Cortez vomited Alexander right out of its belly on a wave of stomach fluid.

"Gross," Winterbottom couldn't help but say.

Global warming may have been slow in coming to Greenland, but it had certainly hit Spain. The country was sweltering, almost uninhabitable. They sat at a sidewalk café table, downing bottles of salty fizzy water and eating tapas. Winterbottom couldn't say the Spanish food agreed with him, but at least the portions were small. He picked at a *tortilla* and sweated, and it was not yet eleven in the morning.

"Where is he?" Alexander said, annoyed.

The two of them were waiting for Juan Francisco Bravo, an old toreador who managed the famed bullring of Pamplona. Bravo had been an acquaintance of the Baddenvaldez branch of the clan. Baddenfields had for centuries been great patrons of the bullfight, the one sport that brought cruelty to the level of an art form.

Winterbottom had tried to cancel the trip. Surely Alexander didn't want to be killed by two different animals on consecutive days. "Besides, you are running out of lives," he said. "You've died twice in just the last forty-eight hours."

"Math, math, math. You always try to scare me with your math. But I'm not planning on dying," Alexander said. "I'm planning on killing that bull. And here's some math for you: I've got five lives left. That's five times as many as you or anyone else on this planet has, including

the bull. We'll be having fresh steak for dinner, just you wait and see."

At least Alexander had allowed Winterbottom to get rid of the scorpion and tarantula, not to mention the python, who was all too happy to go. Only the canal rat seemed sad to get the boot.

"I think that's him," Winterbottom said, looking at the man crossing the plaza toward their table. The aged gentleman was tall and thin and stood ramrod straight. He wore a tight-fitting suit, had a coat draped over one arm, and stabbed at the ground with a thin cane.

"Juan Francisco Bravo, at your service," he said, coming to Alexander and bowing.

"Don Bravo," Alexander said, and actually got up to shake his hand. It was the first time Winterbottom had ever seen the boy polite, let alone impressed. "Is it really true you killed nine hundred sixty-four bulls?"

Bravo waved a hand like it was a magic wand and said, "It is what I do." Winterbottom noted an air of sophistication about Don Bravo which was somewhat intriguing, and somewhat annoying.

"Are you sure you are ready for today, young Baddenfield?" Bravo said. "The first day a boy steps into the bullring—this is the day he becomes a man."

"I'm ready," Alexander said. "I've been practicing a *lot*."

"*Muy bien*," the old master said, and took a sip of the

sangria he had ordered. "Why don't you show me your skills."

Alexander didn't need to be asked twice. He bounced out of his seat and posed still as a statue in matador pose, resplendent in his costume, his rhinestones a-glitter. Juan Francisco Bravo smiled, and everyone on the plaza turned to look at the boy, as if a real bullfight were about to start.

"DUNT dadaDUNT dadaDUNT dadaDUNT-DUNT," Alexander hummed as he whirled around, all red cape and flashing sword. Three times he whisked his cape away at the last second from an imaginary charging bull, and then, for his grand finale, he thrust the cape aside and lunged with his sword, putting the would-be beast to the ground. *"Olé!"* he shouted, and bowed.

During the performance, the people in the plaza rolled their eyes and waved disgustedly as they walked away, while the diners at the sidewalk tapas bar shook their heads and went back to eating. The face of Juan Francisco Bravo, however, turned from tan to pink to boiling red. When Alexander shouted *"Olé!"* a second time, Juan Francisco Bravo slammed his fist on the table, making the glasses and plates jump.

"How dare you!" he thundered, thrusting an accusatory finger to the sky. "You spoiled American brat! What you show me is nothing. It is worse than nothing—it is an insult! The bullfight is an art, a dance. Both weapon

and bull are sacred and must be shown respect by the *torero*!"

"Look, old man," Alexander said, annoyed. "I have the uniform, I have the music, and I have the moves. Let's forget the sacred stuff and get to killing some bulls."

"Ha!" the old matador said, picking himself up from the table. "You are not welcome in my bullring. Go home, *yanqui*!"

Winterbottom knew what was coming next. Another Alexander Moment.

"You old, crotchety, good-for-nothing, too-tight-pants-wearing, nose-stuck-up-in-the-air, Spanish pile of smelly dog *caca*! You are only jealous because you know that Alexander Baddenfield would kill that bull, and faster and better than you ever did, you big phony fraud! You are a chicken! You and your whole country! *Cluck-cluck-cluck!*"

Juan Francisco Bravo replied with a string of phrases in Spanish that we would translate, except we can't, at least not in a book for children, or even young adults. But Don Bravo did add, in English, "You want your bullfight? Fine! You can have your bullfight—and I will cheer for the bull!"

The clocks of the town began to strike—*bong! bong! bong!*—agitating a throb in Winterbottom's head that was only getting worse.

At the arena, the first contestant in the bullring was Guillermo Montezuma, a short, yellow-suited matador from Mexico with a long ponytail, and the second a local favorite wearing royal blue leggings and a matching jacket, Cayatano Filippo Velazquez Ordóñez. After lengthy and cruel prologues, both killed their bulls to *olés* and a shower of roses. The bloody spectacle horrified Winterbottom, but Alexander couldn't get enough. He followed along with his *estoque* and cape, copying every move of the *toreros*.

When his turn came, Alexander strutted into the bullring to the stands-shaking music of the *paso doble*. The purple velvet of his jacket and breeches shimmered in the late afternoon Spanish sun. No one had ever looked more splendid, Alexander was sure. The audience had to be amazed and bedazzled.

But when his name was announced—*El Americano, Alejandro Baddenfield*—boos rained down on the boy instead of *olés*, not to mention overripe tomatoes and eggs. The sound of the crowd only changed when the bull was announced. *Olé! Olé! Olé!*

Alexander was furious.

When it was released, the snorting bull headed straight for the boy. With anger focusing his attention, the fearless Alexander stood his ground even as the hoofbeats of the bull resounded in his chest.

Winterbottom couldn't bear to look. He dropped his head into his hands. The roar of the crowd swelled, then broke in a collective gasp.

The bull had charged right through Alexander's cape and was befuddled to find nothing on the other side. Alexander had executed a perfect pirouette, spinning on his back leg to avoid the bull's charge with the grace of an expert matador.

The bull turned on its heels, and gathered up a good head of steam for a return trip. The crowd cheered him on, then groaned when Alexander again pulled himself away at the last possible instant.

"My goodness," Winterbottom said. "The boy is a natural."

Instead of yanking his cape up at the last minute on the third charge, Alexander pulled it down, as if sweeping the ground. The bull stumbled to its front knees. Seeing his opening, Alexander drew his sword, and was about to stick the bull clean through the neck when the animal jerked its head up and speared a horn through Alexander's side.

Even with deafening cheers rocking the stadium, Winterbottom could hear the cracking of Alexander's ribs, each one like a broomstick being broken over a knee. Then came a sickening pop—Alexander's lung—and another pop—Alexander's other lung.

Alexander's first death had been like a dream; his second, an electric thrill; his third, a surprise so quick he had hardly noticed it; and his fourth, a great big hug. But this, his fifth death, was *horrible*. Not only for the pain—and more pain he had never imagined—but also for the shame and embarrassment, as the bull (whose name was Pelusa, which means "peach fuzz") took a victory lap around the stadium, to *olés* and a rain of roses. But mostly for the pain, as Alexander remained skewered. It grew more and more intense with each leaping, bucking stride the bull took, until, with one great galloping jump, the beast sent Alexander flying to land on the sand in the middle of the ring. As he lay there, in agony, Alexander only wished that he would die.

A few seconds later, his wish came true.

The Sixth Life
of
ALEXANDER BADDENFIELD

lexander was jolted back to life and up onto his feet. He heard the cheers—were they finally for him?

Alas, no. Alexander turned around to see the charging bull nearly upon him. The shock stopped his heart, and he dropped back down to the sand, dead.

The Seventh Life
of
ALEXANDER BADDENFIELD

Alive!
Bull.
Hooves.
Olé!
Dead.

The Eighth Life
of
ALEXANDER BADDENFIELD

The latest life of Alexander began with a jerking recovery of his senses.

"Bull! What? Where?"

But there was no bull. Instead, Alexander was surrounded by a crowd of people, matadors and doctors mostly, talking gibberish. Or rather, Spanish.

"They put the bull back in his pen," Winterbottom said.

"I had a dream while I was dead, Winterbottom," Alexander said. "The bull came back for me, and I was so startled that I had a heart attack, and then I came back to life again just in time to be trampled by him. It was horrible."

Winterbottom and Don Bravo looked at each other.

"That was no *sueño, señorito.*"

"What does that mean, *sueño?*" Alexander asked. "It

was a dream—tell me it was a dream, Winterbottom."

Winterbottom grimly shook his head no, and explained precisely what had happened, in more excruciating detail than Alexander could bear. The boy cut him off.

"How many is that?"

"How many is what?"

"Lives, Winterbottom—*lives*!"

Winterbottom cleared his throat. "Seven."

"Seven?" Alexander said, his eyes going round as baseballs. "*Seven?* Are you sure? That would mean that I only have . . ." He counted *seven, eight, nine* on his fingers. "I only have three lives left!"

"Actually, Alexander," Winterbottom said, and bit his lower lip, "that would mean that you only have two lives left."

"Two?" Alexander's face drooped. "What do you mean, two? You said I was on my seventh life!"

"No, Alexander, I am sorry. I meant to say you have seven lives gone. You are on your *eighth* life."

"You must be wrong. You must have miscounted!"

And so Winterbottom recounted the lives of Alexander Baddenfield, or rather his deaths. By the time he was done, Alexander realized it was true. He had only *one* extra life left.

Alexander felt a chill, his heart began to race, and he felt an emotion he had very little experience with: fear.

And a worse one: uncertainty. How could he live with the uncertainty? Having two lives wasn't much better than having one, now that he knew how deaths could come in bunches. Alexander couldn't risk putting it off. He needed eight new lives right away.

"We have to go to Dr. Kranstenenif's," Alexander said to Winterbottom.

Winterbottom shuddered. "The thought of going back into that strange greenhouse with the frightening menagerie of mixed-up animals gives me the willies."

Winterbottom expected Alexander to make fun of his being nervous (or at least his using the word "willies"), but instead he said, "That's a good point, Winterbottom. I've lost more than half of my lives to animals, and who knows how dangerous those mutant beasts must be."

"And I was so nervous to have to assist him," Winterbottom added. "My hands kept slipping off the tools."

"My god!" Alexander said. "It was madness that I had the operation up there."

"I tried telling you."

"We need to have the operation in New York, in a real hospital, with nurses and gurneys and stuff."

"Hallelujah," Winterbottom said, thrilled Alexander was on his side for once, and immediately began making arrangements to have Kranstenenif flown in to meet them at Baddenfield Castle.

Getting on the plane to fly back home himself, Alexander put on his seat belt as soon as he sat down, and asked the flight attendant to repeat the safety instructions three times. Every tiny knock of turbulence made his heart skip a beat. In the car, Alexander climbed into his old booster seat in the back and kept telling Sam the driver to slow down. "Are you a maniac? Why are you in such a hurry?"

"No hurry, boss kid. This is how I always—"

"Don't talk when you're driving!" Alexander said.

Winterbottom at first took pleasure in watching Alexander frightened into carefulness. But as the boy nervously fidgeted in the booster seat he was much too big for, Winterbottom couldn't help but have the sinking feeling that something had gone horribly wrong.

By the time Dr. Torvic Kranstenenif entered Baddenfield Castle, a mere twenty-four hours after Alexander himself had gotten there, the boy had gone half crazy with hand-wringing and nerves. Only with the buzz of the intercom and the sound of the drawbridge lowering did he relax, his savior having finally arrived. Or had he?

Removed from his arctic lair, Kranstenenif seemed less than before. No longer dressed like a vagabond mad-

man, the scientist wore an old coat and tie that were both too short, and his dandruff-speckled hair lay flat and greasy against his scalp, the tracks of his comb still visible. Rather than dangerous and deranged, Kranstenenif looked shabby. In one hand he carried a black instrument case and in the other a pet carrier, which housed a spotted kitten who was meowing with wide-open mouth and watery blue eyes.

"Boy, am I glad you called, Baddenfield!" Kranstenenif said, shaking the boy's hand like he was hammering a nail. "I tell you, I thought I was going to make a fortune with the whole novavivum-transplant thing. Do you have any idea what you can charge for giving people eight extra lives? Anything you want!" He fell down into an armchair and kicked his legs out in front of him. "But wouldn't you know it? The next three people I tried the surgery on all died right there on the operating table. For *good*."

Alexander's head dropped an inch, and his jaw two inches lower than that.

"I tell you, it's a good thing you wrote me that insurance policy; otherwise me and my rabbitortoise would be homeless on an ice floe somewhere." Kranstenenif shook his head while picking something out of his ear. He looked at whatever it was and wiped it on the armrest.

"So why did the operation work on me?" Alexander said.

"Beats the heck out of me." The scientist shrugged. "Maybe it only works on certain people. Or maybe it was sheer dumb luck. We'll only know if we keep trying!" Kranstenenif opened up his black case and pulled out a stainless-steel surgical saw. He began picking at its teeth.

"Did you ever try the operation on yourself?" Winterbottom asked.

"I may be a mad scientist, but I'm not *crazy*," Kranstenenif said, and let out a *Ha!* "A surgery has to work a few times—in a row—before I'll be going under the knife, thank you very much."

Face turning green, Alexander stammered, "I . . . uhm, I . . ." He looked helplessly at Winterbottom. "I think maybe this is a mistake. I'm not really up for the surgery again."

"What? After I came all this way?" Kranstenenif slumped into his seat like a deflating balloon. Then he perked back up. "I have other ideas, you know. I can make you into a minotaur!"

"A minotaur?"

"Yeah. You'd have the upper body of a bull. Wouldn't that be cool?"

"The *upper* body?" Alexander said. "What about my head?"

Kranstenenif shrugged. "I'll make you a centaur, then. Half man, half horse. Or whatever animal you want on the bottom."

"Look, Doctor," Winterbottom said, getting up, but Kranstenenif cut him off.

"Wait, wait—you're gonna love this one. Are you ready?" Kranstenenif held his thumbs and index fingers at right angles, framing the picture. "I'm going to give you a camel's hump. Think about it: You'll be able to go an entire month without drinking anything!"

It took all the might of Winterbottom and Sam the driver, but they threw Kranstenenif out of the castle, babbling and furious. On Canal Street, no one noticed.

With his newfound fear of dying and no backup lives on the way, Alexander tried returning to the Winterbottom way of doing things. Crossing the street, Alexander looked left, then right, then back left again. But before he could step off the curb, he lost his nerve. What if while he had been looking back left, something happened to the right? It needed to be left, then right, then back left again, then *back right again*. But now he had the same problem. Any number of terrifying vehicles could have come tearing out of nowhere back on the left in the meantime. It was a vicious cycle that never ended.

The outside world contained all kinds of dangers that not even Winterbottom had noticed before, Alexander realized. "Do you see that cloud, Winterbottom? That hideous, threatening cloud?"

Winterbottom looked up. A single cottony cloud hung in the sky, the remnant of a morning storm. He thought it looked like a whale, or perhaps an avocado. "That seems like a perfectly lovely cloud, Alexander."

"Lovely? Sure, if it doesn't strike you down with lightning. It's a menace to have those things hanging over us. The government should start a missile program to shoot them all down." Alexander stopped to think for a moment. "Of course, then there'd be too much sun. That's the real danger. Global warming, skin cancer, the rising seas." Alexander threw up his hands. "The whole sky is just a catastrophe waiting to happen!"

"But remember how you loved it, when you flew with your Icarus wings up above the clouds, up nearly to the sun? And then how you saved yourself, and landed so perfectly? I must say, I was glad you didn't listen to me that day," Winterbottom said. "It was magical."

"Magical?" Alexander said. "It was suicidal!"

Then there were the dogs. All over New York City, canines. It was worse than the African bush! Alexander had to shy away from them on every block.

"Why are you so afraid, Alexander?" Winterbottom said, and even knelt down to pet one of the mongrels.

"You're the one who taught me to steer clear of these things, Winterbottom."

"But I meant pit bulls, Alexander. Not poodles."

"Poodles were *bred* to be vicious."

All Alexander's fears were realized when, walking down Canal Street a few blocks from the castle, a particularly fierce and deceptively small Maltese terrier broke free of its leash and made straight for Alexander. In terror, Alexander fled the other way, only to find himself face-to-face with an obviously rabid, madly barking pug. Trapped between the two yelping dogs, the boy looked for an escape route.

He found himself standing in front of an all-new luxury hotel, with clear glass windows overlooking the sidewalk and a cascading waterfall inside. It looked like paradise, but that glass door! Alexander saw the germs of a thousand hands writhing all over it. He decided to make a break for the street instead, but got caught in the endless left-right-left-right-lefting. Finally, with the two mutts closing in, Alexander had to just go for it.

He had been so preoccupied with looking back and forth for cars that he never saw the bright orange-colored barriers, or the flags, or the enormous WARNING! sign that was right in front of him. As he ran, the ground gave way beneath him, everything went black, and Alexander felt the cold shock of water.

The boy had fallen into an open manhole. He thought he'd landed in the sewer, but it was a drainage canal for storm water. The underground tunnel was still filled from the morning showers, with water rushing fast and whisking Alexander along with it. The boy thought he heard something. His name?

"Alexander! Alexander!" Winterbottom knelt at the opening, calling and calling to nothing but the echo of his own voice and the cool air rising off the water below. Alexander was gone, vanished into the depths of what had to be the sewer, and no doubt getting carried off to some waste management facility. The boy would die a most horrible death—and likely his last!

Winterbottom whipped out his cell phone and hit the tracking app. It showed Alexander moving west under Canal Street. Winterbottom began to run. "*Ooph*, excuse me! *Ooph*, pardon me!" he kept saying, bumping into people. The sidewalk was jammed! The pulsing white dot that was Alexander kept getting farther and farther away. Winterbottom looked for a cab. Canal Street was filled with them—all occupied, stopped bumper-to-bumper, and honking their horns. But then Winterbottom spotted his salvation: a Mr. Rickshaw pedicab coming his way up the bike lane.

Meanwhile, Alexander was experiencing something he hadn't felt since he realized he only had two lives

left: fun. It was like he was on the greatest waterslide in the world! "Ya-hoooo!" he yelled as he hurtled along the underground river.

In the back of the Mr. Rickshaw, Winterbottom chewed his nails. They started gaining on Alexander, but then stopped. Red light. "Go!" Winterbottom yelled to the driver, whose name was Wayne. "The traffic isn't moving—you can sneak right through!"

"No way, dude," Wayne said. "A pedicab has to follow the same laws as a car. I could lose my pedi-hack license!"

Winterbottom reached into his pocket, pulled out a handful of fifty-dollar bills, and shoved them into Wayne's shirt pocket. "Can you follow some different laws, please?"

Wayne's eyes went wide, and he began to weave in and out of traffic and pick up so much speed that Winterbottom got knocked from one side of the pedicab to the other. They began closing in on the Alexander dot, but were almost to the end of Canal Street. Straight ahead was the Hudson River.

Alexander was still laughing and splashing and sliding when he spotted a bright light up ahead. It started as a tiny pinprick of sun, but got wider fast. With a *whoosh* Alexander was whisked out of the underground canal and rode a waterfall down into the Hudson River.

I want to do that again! Alexander thought as he

plunged into the water. Then he remembered that he didn't know how to swim.

Deep in the river, Alexander held his breath and tried to get back to the surface, but once he did, he couldn't stay afloat. He waved with his arms and kicked with his legs, but it was no use. He knew drowning would be a lousy way to die. Had that been life three or four when he had almost drowned? He couldn't quite recall. After breathing in a few more gulps of seawater, he couldn't recall anything at all.

The Ninth Life
of
ALEXANDER BADDENFIELD

No amount of fifty-dollar bills could help Winterbottom cross the West Side Highway. Traffic was streaming fast in both directions, and he had to wait at a red light for what seemed like forever. Was it broken?

Looking down at his phone, he saw that the dot that was Alexander had stopped moving, right at the edge of the Hudson. Oh, why had he never taught Alexander how to swim!

Finally the light turned green, the cars on the highway stopped, and Winterbottom sprinted through the crosswalk into the river park to the railing, where he immediately saw Alexander floating.

Winterbottom dove over the side and quickly had the boy in a lifeguard carry, Alexander's head up under the crook of his arm, as he swam to the marina. Had Winterbottom gotten to him in time? He wasn't breathing, but maybe if Winterbottom got him back to the dock and gave him CPR, he could revive Alexander before he wasted another life and—

"Is that you, Winterbottom?" Alexander said, lifting his head. Then he coughed out a gallon of seawater.

The final life of Alexander Baddenfield started differently from all the others. Alexander felt no exhilarating jolt, no thrill at his very aliveness. Instead, he felt queasy. Back home, he examined himself in the mirror. His skin looked pale, almost green, and black circles ringed his eyes.

"What if I've contracted some horrible disease and I don't even know it?" he said. "What if my last life just started and I'm already dying?"

"But Alexander, you are brand-new!" Winterbottom said.

"Except I just took a ride in a sewer! Think of the billions of germs that must have been in there. I could have typhoid fever or some sort of Chinese spider monkey disease."

"But it wasn't a sewer; it was a storm drain," Winterbottom said. "That was all fresh water."

"Well, what about the Hudson River then? Can you think of anything more polluted than a river running between Manhattan and New Jersey?"

The only sensible thing, Alexander decided, was never to leave Baddenfield Castle again. It was too risky to even step out onto the sidewalk.

"You had the right idea all along, Winterbottom, keeping me locked up in here."

"But it was too much, Alexander," Winterbottom said. "You can't become like me. For a Baddenfield to be cautious upsets the natural order of things."

As ever, Alexander refused to listen, and shrank further and further behind the moated walls of Baddenfield Castle. He ordered every window boarded up to keep out the dangerous sun, and still he put on sunblock. No outside air was allowed to enter the building, so fresh oxygen had to be pumped in. Alexander refused all nuts, all dairy, and everything else on Winterbottom's old dietary restrictions list, and then refused some more. He stopped eating anything anyone anywhere had ever been allergic to. The more Alexander read on the Internet, the more he discovered that the problem was food itself. *Any* food can kill you. So Alexander just stopped eating altogether.

The boy spent more and more time in the Hall of Baddenfields, mulling over what had happened to his ancestors, and himself.

"When you're down to your last life and you're wishing you had this one back, just remember who told you so," Alexander repeated to Winterbottom. "That's what you said, and I do remember. Oh, do I remember." He shook his head and turned away from the portraits. "You were right, Winterbottom. So, so right."

No one had ever been so sorry to be proved correct. In fact, Winterbottom couldn't bear to hear the boy repeat it. "Please, Alexander, just leave this room of lives and deaths and go outside and play like a twelve-year-old is supposed to!"

Alexander looked at Winterbottom as if he were crazy and snorted.

"What is the point of living this last life if you have no fun?" Winterbottom said. "You are no worse off than you were before you started all this. You were born with one life and one life is what you have now, the same as I have, the same as everyone has!"

"It's totally different. Your glass is still full. Mine is eight-ninths empty." Alexander shook his head. "You've got no idea what it's like to have had so many lives."

While Alexander spoke, Winterbottom had an epiphany. He became excited, and realized that he had hit upon the answer. Not just to Alexander's plight, but to that of all the Baddenfields who had come before him. All he had to do was explain it to him, and the boy would be *convinced*.

"This is where it could all be different for you, Alexander," Winterbottom said. "This could be your Hollywood ending, your happily-ever-after. You could leave this room right this instant, shut the door forever, and decide that one life is life enough, and that you will live it your own way. You could say, 'Alexander Baddenfield, the last of the Baddenfields, is no more. He is instead Alexander Not-So-Baddenfield, who hopes to become Alexander Goodenfield, if not one day Alexander Very-Bestenfield.' The Baddenfield curse isn't about dying, but the horrible mess you Baddenfields have made of living. All you have to do, Alexander," Winterbottom said, and took the boy's gaunt face in his hands, "is say, *I will change*, unlock yourself from this house, and go out and live your one life."

Alexander Baddenfield listened to everything that was said by Winterbottom, the only friend he had ever had. He thought it over, and said, "You've watched too many movies."

But Winterbottom didn't flinch or back down. "If you don't change, Alexander Baddenfield, I swear to you that I will pack my bags right now, walk out of this house, and leave you forever."

"You won't leave," Alexander said. Not out of spite, or out of meanness, or as a dare, but because he knew it to be true.

"You are wrong, Alexander. You think you're not, but you are."

"You won't leave," Alexander said. "You can't. You are a Winterbottom, and I am a Baddenfield, and that's that."

"Well, that's not that for me, not anymore." Winterbottom wished he had a hat to put on, because putting on a hat in a huff would have made his exit more emphatic, or at least an overcoat through which to angrily stick his arms, but as he had neither, he simply stomped out. He quickly threw some clothes into a suitcase, grabbed his toothbrush, and marched down the stairs.

The drawbridge hummed as it lowered over the moat, that last stretch of canal from Dutch New Amsterdam, and revealed to Winterbottom the perfect New York autumn day, the kind that those Indians who sold their island for $24 in knickknacks must have dreamed about for years after they left. It had been so many weeks since he'd seen the sun, there in boarded-up Baddenfield Castle, that Winterbottom had forgotten what a beautiful day was like.

Or had he never allowed himself to notice them in the first place? So terrified of losing the last of the Baddenfields had Winterbottom been that he had smothered the boy. Otherwise, Alexander would not have been so desperate to test the limits he had set, or returned to them so ferociously. Winterbottom could only blame

himself for what had happened, and his greatest fear being nearly realized—Alexander's final death—wasn't even the worst part. It was that the boy could no longer face it. Alexander, whose bravery had been his single good quality, no longer had even that.

With slumped shoulders, Winterbottom walked back inside Baddenfield Castle without even having set foot on the drawbridge.

The final end came quickly for Alexander.

By the time it did, his bubble of self-pity and worry had turned into a literal bubble. Having realized that the old castle itself was surely killing him with lead paint, asbestos, and black mold, Alexander had ordered his room to be sealed in plastic. Winterbottom was the only person allowed in, and even then only after he had gone through the antibacterial shower that Alexander had gotten from Dr. Kranstenenif in exchange for back rent. His only other companion was his cat.

"Shaddenfrood, you dumb animal, don't you know how fragile life is? How easy it is to die? It hardly even takes trying," Alexander said. "You have all of one measly life left, and yet you lie there, purring—actually purring!—without a thought that one wrong turn and it's the end!"

All too soon, Alexander developed a sniffle that never

got any better. His eyes began to get itchy and water, the sniffle expanded into a cold, and he became ill. All the doctors he had earlier visited now paid him house calls— the second-best doctor in the world, the third-best, the fourth-best, and so on—but none of them could say what was wrong with the boy.

When he felt the first shadowy chill of death that he had felt eight times before, Alexander abandoned his last shred of pride and had Winterbottom call the first-best doctor in the world.

Dr. Sorrow examined the boy, and reexamined him just to make sure his diagnosis was correct. He then put his stethoscope back in his bag and shook his head. "Alexander, you poor, wretched boy," he said. "By shutting yourself off from the world and all the natural things that keep us healthy, you have developed the most acute case of *felis domesticitis* I have ever seen."

"Felis . . . domestic . . . itis . . . ?" Alexander said weakly. "What is it?"

"An allergy to the common house cat," Dr. Sorrow replied.

Winterbottom stifled a sob; Alexander closed his eyes and nodded.

The doctor showed himself out, while Winterbottom whisked up the cat to remove him.

"No," Alexander said. "It's too late."

"But maybe it isn't."

"If there's one person who knows when it's too late, it's me. Just one thing, Winterbottom," Alexander said, and it took all the energy he had left just to ask the question. "What is your first name?"

"Why, it's Winter, of course," he said, taken aback. "My name is Winter Bottom the Eighteenth."

Alexander smiled and maybe even laughed. If he did, it was with the final breath he ever took, for the last of the Baddenfields was dead.

Forever.

A quietly weeping Winterbottom picked the boy's body up in his arms and lifted it off the bed. Alexander was as light as a feather. Was it possible that there was one life left in him? Maybe he really hadn't drowned in the Hudson. Winterbottom gently shook the boy, hoping that he would spring back to life and say something horribly obnoxious. He didn't.

As Winterbottom left the room with the body, Shaddenfrood jumped onto Alexander's bed and curled up in the faint hollow that his master had left. The spot was still warm, and it felt lovely. Shaddenfrood purred.

THE END

❧

Well, that sure was a sappy ending! I can't believe I went out like such a wimp. What was I so worried about anyway? Being dead is cool. Mad cool.

Alexander kept telling himself that, but he didn't know what being dead for good was really like. The only other time he had really been dead—*dead* dead—was that first time, when he'd died on the operating table and watched Kranstenenif operate on him from above. This time he saw Winterbottom carry out his dead body and Shaddenfrood leap up on his bed. That made him smile. Shaddenfrood was a Baddenfield. But so were most cats.

The thing was, he just kept watching the same boring thing—his bedroom. It occurred to Alexander that maybe this was all there was after death: your spirit watching over the spot where you died for the rest of eternity. He should've died the last time somewhere more interesting. Like the bullring.

Just as Alexander was getting really bored, a change came over him. He began to feel something. Could he be coming back to life? Had he somehow miscounted?

But it wasn't his old body he was feeling. It was his spirit, and it was getting heavier. It began to sink.

Down through the floor of his room.

Down through the basement of Baddenfield Castle.

Down through the subway.

Down.

Down.

Down.

And although he was probably just imagining it, he couldn't shake the feeling that things were beginning to get just the teensiest bit warm.

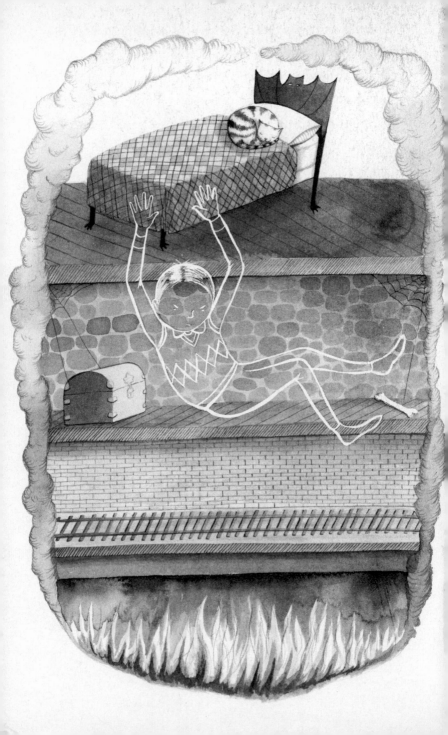